W9-CYS-392

A HISTORY MYSTERY
by David Mark Lopez

To: Bridget, Christina, Laura, Gail, Curt & Bobi
for inspiration, editing and proofreading.

Orange Marker Episode **4**

Fly
Like a Witch

Maddie's Magic Markers

by David Mark Lopez

Maddie's Magic Marker Series
Orange Marker (Four)
Fly Like a Witch
Copyright 2007 by David Mark Lopez
ISBN 10: 0-9744097-3-1
ISBN 13: 978-0-9744097-3-3
Library of Congress Control Number:2007902623

Published by David Mark Lopez
Bonita Springs, FL

All rights reserved. No part of this publication may be reproduced or stored in a retrieval system or transmitted in any form by means of electronic, mechanical, photocopy, recording or by wire without permission of the publisher as provided by USA copyright law.

Story and Illustrations by David Mark Lopez
Cover Illustration/Book Design by Eileen Laibinis
Printed in the United States of America

What Kids, Parents and Teachers Are Saying About Maddie's Magic Markers!

"I recently found and purchased your first book in the series at a home school book event in Orlando. My seven year old son was studying Ancient Egypt at the time and I thought he would really enjoy your book. WOW! He began to read it and didn't stop until he read it from cover to cover!"
-*Christine*

"I received a phone call from my grandchildren in Hawaii, who after reading your book, requested more in the series. They were totally enthralled and can't wait to read more."
-*Jeanette*

"My students really enjoyed your book talk last month. They have been discussing your books and reading them ever since. Thanks so much for getting them excited about reading."
-*Janet, 5th Grade Teacher*

"I liked the part where the guy shoots the bear."
-*Jason, 4th Grade*

"Usually I don't like history, but with your books, history couldn't be any easier !!"
- *Lily, 3^d Grade*

"Are you really related to Jennifer Lopez?"
-*Cesar, 4th Grade*

"Your books are funny, kid-friendly and delightful historical fiction."
-*Maria, 5th Grade*

Maddie's Magic Markers were written, illustrated and published by its author, David Mark Lopez. Maddie's Magic Markers is intended to be a series of twelve historical adventures. If you have any comments or questions about the books, or have suggestions for Maddie's future travels, please contact the author. He can be reached by phone at 239 947 2532, by mail at 3441 Twinberry Court, Bonita Springs, FL 34134 or by e-mail at www.davidmarklopez.com He would love to know what you think of the books. If you would like to order additional copies of either book, simply fill out the form below and mail it along with your check or money order.

Name:_____

Address:_____

Phone #:_____

E-mail address:_____

Please send me_____copies of
Walk Like an Egyptian @ 6:00 per copy
(includes tax, postage and handling)

Please send me_____copies of
Ride Like an Indian @ 6:00 per copy
(includes tax, postage and handling)

Please send me_____copies of
Run Like a Fugitive @ 6:00 per copy
(includes tax, postage and handling)

Please send me_____copies of
Fly Like a Witch @ 6:00 per copy
(includes tax, postage and handling)

Mail to:

David Mark Lopez
3441 Twinberry Court
Bonita Springs, FL 34134

Table of Contents

Table of Contents
(continued)

Chapter 1
BOO!

Dad's top three incredibly boring Halloween stories:

One: When he was little, Dad and his older brother (Uncle Kenny) would go trick-or-treating around their neighborhood, figure out which houses were handing out the best candy, go back home and change masks. Then these juvenile delinquents in training went back to the houses that had the best candy for a double dip. Just wrong.

Two: Because his family was so poor, Dad never EVER got candy for any occasion except Halloween. So to make his candy last he would only eat one piece a day until it was gone, saving the disgusting orange and black candy caramels until everything else was gone. On a good year he could make the candy last until Christmas. Pathetic.

Three: Because his father was an independent Baptist preacher, Dad was required to go to church on Sunday nights. Naturally one year, Halloween fell on a Sunday night. Dad's brilliant strategy that year was to go trick-or-treating the night before Halloween, on Saturday night. Whenever I try to picture Dad dressed up as whatever he was that year, going house to house, like some kind of moron who forgot what day Halloween actually was, it cracks me up. He said he didn't get much candy that year, but did receive lots of funny looks. Really? Embarrassing.

Ok, maybe these stories aren't so boring, but maybe after you heard them every Halloween for the past 10 years you would be sick of them just like I am. Of course Dad's favorite holiday is Halloween. He starts decorating the house in early October and spends the whole month dressing up like the Phantom of the Opera and trying to jump out from behind stuff (any nearby tree, dresser or dark place will do) and scare the jellybeans out of you.

"Boo!"

"Hi, Dad."

"Did I scare you?"

"No. Hey, Mr. Scary Phantom of the Opera."

"What?"

"Your pants are unzipped."

"Uh-oh. How do you like the cape?"

"Very nice. Thanks, Dad."

"For what?"

"For not singing."

You've probably figured out this is Maddie again. Hi! It's been awhile since my last horrible adventure and lots of things have happened that I need to update you on. I am now twelve and a half. The good news is that I will be a teenager in no time. Yay! The bad news is that every time my dad sees a goofy looking boy he asks me if that is my boyfriend. Not funny. The other big event is that we moved from the thriving metropolis of McIntosh, Florida to Bonita Springs, Florida - world's capital for old people. If you like black socks with sandals and German tourists wearing their swimming suits in the grocery store, Bonita is the place for you. On the plus side our house is much bigger and I finally have a room of my own. Of course that doesn't stop Thing One, Natalie, and Thing Two, Brett, from coming into my room every thirty seconds to bother me. Unfortunately neither one of them has grasped the concepts of PRIVACY and PERSONAL PROPERTY. But since I only have to put up with them part-time, I will have mercy on them.

I've pretty much decided that I'm never going to use my markers again after my last disastrous trip. In fact, since we've moved I don't even really know where they are. Who cares? The only thing the markers have gotten me is bitten by a crocodile (rest in peace, Steve Irwin), falsely accused, slimed by a cobra, nearly drowned, treed by a psychotic bear, devoured by mosquitoes, frozen to death, kidnapped by Indians, scratched and gnawed by rats, chased by soldiers, hunted by dogs and locked in a very small closet. Oh yeah, and nearly choked to death by an assassin. Other than that it was all just a bunch of non-stop fun. No more markers for me. Thanks, but no thanks.

Dad's birthday is also in October, so since he was turning 45 he came up with the brilliant idea that we would go mountain climbing in the White Mountains in New Hampshire. That's right, mountain climbing. Has Dad ever climbed a mountain? Maybe a mountain of ice cream complete with nuts and hot fudge. This could only end badly, but since it was his birthday I indulged him and went along. He probably couldn't get anyone else to go. No way was the Stepmonster going hiking and camping out.

Anyway it turned out to be way better than I expected. Dad flew up to Atlanta and then we both flew from there to Boston. The only bad part is that I forgot my i-pod, so I had to listen to Dad's ridiculous music that he gets from his weirdo friend, Steve, who actually looks normal but in reality is a music geek. Take a scroll through Dad's i-pod and let me know if you have ever even heard of any of these bands: My Bloody Valentine, the Stills, Dead Boy and the Elephantmen, Arcade Fire, the Wrens, Built to Spill, the Doves, Flaming Lips, The Whigs, My Morning Jacket...shall I go on? Only Dad, Steve and three other people have ever heard any of this music. It probably has been banned from any and all radio stations. Time for some fun.

"Hey, Dad."
"Whaaaadddduppppp, dog."
"Dad, no one says that anymore."
"I just did."
"Exactly. Anyway."
"What?"
"Have you heard the new CD by the Paperclips?"
"No, is it good?'
"Dad, I just made that up. There is no band named the Paperclips."
"There should be."

When we finally got to Boston, Uncle Chris and Auntie Christina picked us up. These people aren't really my relatives, but they are actually way more fun. They aren't even Dad's friends (Dad doesn't have any friends of his own, he just borrows everyone

9

else's). Christina was the Stepmonster's roommate in college and Chris, her husband, was going to be our mountain climbing guide. We stayed at their house for a couple of days and Auntie Christina took us sightseeing.

We visited the nearby town of Salem and took in the Witch Museum (nothin' but cheese) and the House of the Seven Gables. Let me give you fair warning if you ever go to the House of the Seven Gables with my dad and you ask him why the ceilings are so low and he tells you that people were much shorter back then, don't believe him. About 10 seconds after he fed me this lie, our guide said that the ceilings were low to preserve energy and keep the houses warm in the winter. I kicked him. One cool thing about that house is that it had a mysterious secret stairway. All in all it was a fun day. Tightwad Dad even coughed up some money for some of the country's oldest candy (lemon Gibraltars that melt in your mouth) and a t-shirt at the Witch Museum. I shoved a packet of candy in my pocket.

The next day was mountain climbing. Oh boy! Uncle Chris got us up early and we stopped at Dunkin' Donuts. Uncle Chris says you can't swing a dead cat in Boston without hitting a Dunkin' Donuts. Then we drove for awhile up to New Hampshire. We stopped and looked at the Old Man in the Mountain and I'm glad we did, because it fell apart a few months later.

We finally parked, packed up all of our gear and started up the mountain. The plan was to hike up Mount Clinton, spend the night at the Appalachian Mountain Club Hut, Mizpah Springs, and hike up some more mountains the next day. Actually since Dad was carrying all my gear it was pretty easy. It's about 3800 feet up to the hut and the climbing wasn't too bad. Mostly like going up stairs in hiking boots. About ten minutes after we started going up, we hit snowfall. It made the climbing a little harder, but I had to admit it was beautiful. The snow falling on the pines was simply spectacular. I thought I was hiking through a Christmas card. Even more fun was hitting Dad in the head with a snowball. No way was he catching me with that heavy pack.

It only took us about an hour and a half to get to the hut. It was still early and we felt so good we decided to drop our gear off and keep climbing. We climbed Mount Jackson and had some amazing panoramic views of Mount Washington and the rest of the Presidential Range. We had enough climbing for one day, so we trudged back to the hut.

These AMC huts are more like big lodges with no electricity or fire places. We put our stuff away in our bunks (everyone sleeps together) and went back to the great room. Dad taught me how to play backgammon and I beat him about six straight times. After a hearty dinner provided by the people who run the hut, the guides gave us a "safety talk' and demonstrated how to get an injured person off of the mountain. I guess the big deal around here is trying not to twist your ankle or freeze to death since the temperature can change so rapidly. They call that hypothermia. I got to be the guinea pig, and so they strapped me on a mountain stretcher and pretended to take me down the mountain. Dad showed me the hut library and the journal kept by all the other hikers who had come before us. I looked over a couple of the books, and then we went back downstairs. We talked to all the other climbers that were spending the night in the hut.

Since there is no electricity, we pretty much had to go to bed when it got dark. Uncle Chris loaned me his miner's headlight to wear, in case I had to get up in the middle of the night to go pee. Fortunately I only had to do this once right before I went to sleep. It must have been about 40 degrees because when I got back to my sleeping bag I was shivering and my teeth were chattering. I thought I heard a wolf howling, but Dad said all the wolves around here were long gone and the only thing to worry about on these mountains here were bears and to stop jabbering and go to sleep. Thanks, Dad. I dreamed I was being attacked by bears, but it was only Dad's championship snoring.

The next morning we got up, dressed quickly and tried to warm up. You could see your breath INSIDE the hut. Some hot breakfast made things better and everyone sang, "Happy Birthday" to Dad and he had a special birthday pancake with a candle. Then

11

we finished putting on our fleece, water-proof jackets and hiking boots and headed out for more vertical climbing. It was harder than the day before because we were closer to the summit and it was much steeper. Of course it started snowing again just to make things a little harder. We finally made it to the top of Mount Clinton (4310 feet). Everyone felt great, so we decided to try for one more peak before we headed back down to the hut and then home. We headed for Mount Eisenhower (4780 feet). That doesn't sound much higher, but first we had to go back down part of Mount Clinton, before we could go back up. When we got above the tree line the wind and the snow were really blowing. There were snowdrifts up to my thighs and the visibility was so low we could barely see the cairns (rock piles) guiding our way to the top.

I didn't think we were going to make it, but Uncle Chris and Dad kept plugging along and we finally reached the top. The wind must have been blowing at about fifty m.p.h., so we quickly took a couple of pictures and headed back down. We got back to the hut two hours later, had some yummy soup and got ready to hike back to our vehicle at the bottom of the mountain.

We were outside the hut and just underway when I remembered I wanted to write something in the library journal.

"Hey, Dad, wait up!"
"What?"
"I forgot to write something in the journal. Can you hold up a minute?"
"Ok, but make it snappy. We want to get back down before dark."
"No problem."
"Here, Maddie. Take this in case they don't have anything to write with."

He tossed me an orange pen. I caught it and scrambled back to the hut, jumped the steps and ran up the stairs to the library. I opened the journal and pulled off the orange cap of the pen. I started writing down who we were and about the three mountains we climbed. For some reason the orange marker reminded me of

Halloween and that funny song about a pumpkin we learned at a Halloween party at the library when I was little:

> I'm orange and round,
> Got a nose and a mouth
> And a candle in my belly.
> My head pops off when ever I want (popping noise),
> And some people think I'm scary.
> Boo!

Oddly, I started getting drowsy, and thought I smelled something like popcorn balls and candy corn. I took a hard look at the pen and realized the odor was coming from the marker tip, and the ink floating in the glass part of the pen was glowing like some kind of phosphorescent liquid. Uh-oh. My head started spinning and I tilted off the chair. I steadied myself, abandoned my journal entry, exited the hut, and sprinted down the mountain to catch up with Dad and Uncle Chris. That dopey song was still playing in my head, the dizziness returned, and there stood my dad wearing his ridiculous cape and giving me the thumbs up sign. I know I heard the long, slow, mournful cry of a wolf in the snowy distance.

Chapter 2

NOT BY THE HAIR OF MY CHINNY-CHIN-CHIN

Maddie's top five rules for time travel:

1. First, don't panic. Take a few minutes and several deep breaths to get your bearings. Then panic.

2. Try to figure out where in the world you are. There appears to be absolutely no rhyme or reason to where the markers decide to drop me. Head for anything that remotely appears like civilization. Not as easy as it sounds.

3. Try to find someone famous. This will help you find out what period of History you landed in. What will it be this time? Cave men, pirates, circus performers, spies, head-hunters, aliens? How 'bout a really cute football team? Doubtful. Even better: a shopping mall!

4. Avoid being eaten, imprisoned, drowned, frozen, burned, kidnapped, stabbed, shot, knifed, or otherwise murdered.

5. Find the magic bead and get yourself home.

Oh yeah, I forgot the most important one: KILL DAD FOR GIVING YOU THESE INSANE MAGIC MARKERS!!!!

A cold, gray, steely dawn stretched out in front of me with ribbons of pink and orange dramatically rising as each minute slowly passed. It was definitely cold. My breath was making little smoke signals. Thank goodness I was still wrapped in my fleece pullover and my down jacket. My hiking boots were snug and tight. I wasn't going to freeze to death. So far, so good.

I appeared to be in a pretty thick forest that rose and fell around me in an irregular layout. I started hiking up a hill that gradually got steeper to get a better view. The squirrels ran and chittered ahead of me with the early morning news. The trees were bare and the dead leaves crunched under my deliberate steps. I skidded on the occasional patch of snow. At first I tried not to make too much noise, but it was nearly impossible with all the underbrush, so I gave up. As usual, I thought I heard something in the background, but whenever I stopped to listen carefully I heard only the chirping of some early birds. Good luck with those frozen worms, guys.

There was a clearing at the top of the hill, and I picked my way around some rocks and boulders to get to the top. When I saw the smoke rising from some distant buildings I knew I was on the right track. Those buildings were hopefully only about a mile or two away. I could already taste the crispy bacon and the scrambled eggs. I turned and started down the hill. This was almost too easy. Dad would call this a "moderate climb." If it wasn't for my heavy boots, I'd be skipping right now.

The snarling, gray, one hundred pound eastern timber wolf standing smack dab in the middle of the path took my breath away. He was magnificent. The grizzled fur on his back was standing straight up and he was hunkered down with his forelegs splayed out in front of him. Time stood still while I remembered what I had read about wolves in the Mizpah Springs library. *Canus Lupus Lycaon once roamed from New England to the Great Lakes. White Mountains Survival Guide, Vol. I, p. 37.*

His hypnotic light-blue eyes were locked on mine in a prehistoric stare-down. When was the last time this guy had a good meal? *Food: large hoofed animals such as deer and elk and occasionally smaller animals, WMSG, p.38.*

Uh, that would be...me. Trouble in doggie land. I slowly started turning my body in anticipation of a full-blown sprint down the hill to who knows where? The low-throated growl gurgling from his throat was both impressive and bone chilling.

Without moving my body any more, I pain stakingly turned my head and took in my surroundings. *Wolves live and hunt in packs. A hierarchy of dominate and subordinate members within the pack assist it to operate as a unit. Wolves talk to each other by vocalizations, facial expressions and body postures, WMSG, p.40.*

My slow 180 degree head-turn revealed two slightly smaller females on either side of me, one ghostly white and the other black and gray, both about twenty yards away. Almost on cue, Alpha Male directly in front of me threw his head back and let loose a blood-curdling howl that made my bones ache.

During his primal scream, in stop action photography, I stooped down and picked up the biggest rock my trembling fingers could find. In one motion, I stood and fired a side-armed missile aimed right between Whitefang's glacier-blue eyes. He dodged the stone effortlessly, but it gave me the two seconds I needed to make my death scamper down the hill. "Wolf Family United" followed in deadly pursuit. *An adult, male timber wolf can reach speeds upward of 35-40 mph during a chase, WMSG, p.41.* These silent, efficient hunters wasted not one single ounce of energy barking, snarling or otherwise indicating just how close they were. Sheer, blind terror drove me forward.

I instantly recognized this wasn't anything like escaping from dim-witted dogs. These top-of-the food-chain mammals were professional killers, the hit-men of the animal kingdom. The only incredibly slim chance I had for survival was to get somewhere they couldn't reach me. The slightest mistake doomed me. Survival instinct alone guided me.

Out of my peripheral vision I spied potential salvation when I reached the bottom of the hill. A sheer rock wall jutted out from a thick glade about thirty yards to my right. I made the sharpest right turn I've ever made in my life and felt a snapping wolf glance off my back. I nearly lost my balance, but I sprinted toward the wall with wolves keeping step on both sides of me, Hell's finest escort service. Ten seconds to go, with a fortuitous tree-line of hardwoods on both sides saving my life every step of the way.

Three feet before I leaped for the wall, the ghost wolf darted between two saplings and ripped my snow pants and threw me off balance. I hit the wall sideways, but somehow managed to find a grip with my left hand, and kicked off another wolf as I slammed into the granite face of the cliff. I desperately clawed the air for another handhold, kicking snarling and flailing wolves out of mid-air. Somehow my right hand miraculously found another outcropping and I hauled myself upward. One flying desperado leaped from a nearby boulder, locking his death-grip jaws on my right boot. I tried to shake him free, but he just wouldn't let go. I strengthened my grip and slammed him into the wall about six times before he finally gave it up. My adrenalin took over and I finally scrambled up to safety about twenty feet up. I was shocked to see at least twelve wolves impatiently, silently, pacing the ground below. They definitely weren't used to seeing their quarry get away. No sign of "Steroid Wolf", but who cared? I stood up, punched both fists into the air and screamed into the frosty, morning air. Take that, wolf pack. If you need some breakfast, try Dunkin' Donuts.

I never saw the big, bad wolf coming. He silently leaped through the frozen dawn, slamming into my right shoulder with all of his massive, one hundred pounds. Kablooie! I had absolutely no chance of keeping my feet. My house of straw collapsed, and I fell headlong off the cliff into the pack of hungry, grinning wolves. I managed to roll forward as I fell, but an unimaginable, sharp pain pierced my knee as I hit the ground. The wolves surrounded me immediately in a feeding frenzy, silently tearing my swaddling clothes to pieces. In mere seconds they would be at my vital organs, ripping me to bloody shreds. I did the best I could just to cover my head. So this is what it feels like to be eaten alive. Black death hovered over me, reaching out. I just never knew he wore a cape.

Chapter 3
NOT EXACTLY APRIL IN PARIS

In my dream I am flying. Flying not like a bird where I have to flap my wings like crazy just to stay aloft, but in this dream I am soaring. My arms are straight behind me, my black dress flutters in the wind, and I fly over the mountains, down the valleys, over farms, rooftops, churches, fields. I never land. I just keep going and going until I reach the ocean and then I fly up and down the beach and then out, out to dark blue sea.

I woke up with a start when the door opened and I fell into the person who opened it? As I fell inward the excruciating pain in my knee made me groan.

"Why, child, what is the matter? Elizabeth, come quickly!"

The man in the dark suit, picked me up and cradled me in his arms.

"Please, please help me. I was attacked by wolves... and there's something terribly wrong with my knee."

"Why...why, who are you and how in heaven's name did you get here?"

I was just about to pass out again, but he shook me. Really hard.

"I don't know...I mean my name is Maddie, but I don't know how I got here. It seemed like I was flying."

He raised an eyebrow, and I noticed he was staring intently at my clothes.

"Samuel, close that door and bring the poor child in here, before she freezes to death."

As he lifted me up, I blacked out again from the pain.

When I came to, I was in a bed and it was dark. I was out of my hiking clothes and dressed in something that had to be a nightgown. I was warm and my knee was bandaged tightly. It still hurt, but not like before. I felt around for all my body parts and everything was still there. I had a few cuts and bruises, but I had somehow survived both my fall and the wolves. I was alive, but I had no idea of how I got here. In fact, I had no idea of where "here" was.

I overheard whispering voices in the next room.

"Elizabeth, it is simply impossible. There is no way we can afford to take on another person in this household. We already have my niece, Abigail, to take care of. You realize of course, that it has now been two years since I was last paid for my services."

"But Samuel, what can we do with her?. She came to us in need."

"She didn't 'come' to us in anything. I just opened the door and she fell in. That doesn't make her our responsibility."

"But, Samuel."

"I will hear nothing more of this matter. We'll...we'll just have to find out where she came from and send her back."

Louder now.

"But what about the...Indians ...the wolves? The poor child doesn't even know how she got here."
"Enough!"
Practically yelling, like Dad.

I somehow managed to pull my swollen leg out of bed and stood up and reached for the wall. I hopped along the wall across a cold, bare floor and pushed the heavy, wooden door open. The man and the woman who had been arguing looked embarrassed. They looked at each other and then looked back at me.

"Well, good morning, Miss Maddie, how are you feeling? I am the Reverend Samuel Parris and this is my wife, Goody Elizabeth. You may not remember this, but we found you at our doorstep last night, when I went out to get some wood."

"The" Reverend? Goody? Nice and slow.

"...I do, I do remember. At least a little. Thanks for taking care of me and wrapping up my knee. I think it's feeling a little better today."

"Perhaps we can have Doctor Griggs come and take a look at you later on. But now, I need to ask you a few questions."

I didn't really have a good feeling about the Rev. He looked kind of spooky and I'm pretty sure about ten minutes ago he was yelling at his wife about how to get rid of me. Now he was all happy and smiling. But also a little fidgety and twitchy. He had this weird way of rubbing his hands together when he was talking. His wife seemed nice enough, but I decided to play it safe before I told him too much.

"So, Maddie?"

He paused and sucked in a deep, long breath through his crooked teeth.

"Where are you visiting from?"
"Uh.." Ok let's try this, "...Boston."
"My, my. You are certainly a long way from home. How did you make it all the way up here to visit us in Salem Village?"

21

Salem Village? Salem! SALEM! My mind started calculating. This room was cold and lit by a fireplace. I saw some half burnt, glowing candles nearby. No electricity. Nobody wore clothes like the ones these people were wearing unless they were headed to a funeral. Plain, simple furniture. Definitely the wrong century. Keep thinking! Keep thinking!" I hesitated.

"I'm...not...sure."

"Well, you told us when you arrived that perhaps you flew here. Is that true?"

His head jerked.

Of course, I flew here, but it was on an airplane, dimwit. Probably not a good idea to let Reverend Twitchy know I was from the future and that there, people flew thousands of miles in shiny, silver tubes with wings that didn't move.

"Reverend Parris, I really can't remember much except the wolves attacking me."

He stroked his chin and stared at me with pale, blue eyes. More hand rubbing.

"What about those unusual clothes you were wearing? I suppose you don't know anything about those either?"

A sinister grin. I shrugged my shoulders and gave him my best "Who me?" look. I decided to change the subject.

"Mr., I mean Reverend Parris, can I ask you a question?"

He nodded slowly.
"What day is this?"
"It is Saturday."
"No, I mean what date?"
"December 2nd."

"The year?"

"The year? It's the year of our Lord, sixteen-hundred and ninety-one. Such an odd question."

Sixteen hundred and ninety one.., 1691. .1691! Salem, Massachusetts. Oh, my goodness. No pizza, no television, no brownies, no cheeseburgers. No shopping malls. No United States of America. No electricity. No nothin'. Terrific. I slowly brought my attention back to Samuel Parris who continued to eye me suspiciously. I decided to stick with the "amnesia" routine.

"I just can't remember anything except climbing in the mountains and being chased by the wolves."

"Well, where exactly is your family in Boston?"

I shrugged my shoulders again..

"Well, we can't very well send you back to Boston until you remember where you came from and until your knee gets better. Perhaps a little honest work will heal both your knee and your memory. You can stay here for the time being, but tomorrow I am going to see if anyone in the church needs a hard-working girl."

Ok, that didn't sound like much fun, but it was way too early to spill the beans about my time-traveling. I needed a lot more information before I could come up with a plan. He spun on his heels and walked away, indicating that this conversation was officially over.

"Uh, Reverend Parris?"

He sighed in an exasperated manner.

"Yes?"

"I think it would be helpful if I could talk to someone famous."

"Famous?"

"You know, well-known. Somebody everyone looks up to, and that everybody knows."

He threw back his head and cackled and little drops of spit flew everywhere. Take it easy, big boy.

"I suppose I'm the only one around here who would meet that description. Of course, since YOU are from Boston you surely know Cotton Mather?"

"Not, really."

"Cotton Mather is the minister of Boston's North Church and one of the leaders of our Puritan Church. Perhaps you are familiar with his recent book, *Memorable Providences Relating to Witchcraft*, the unfortunate story of the Goodwin children?"

He leaned in so close I could smell his rancid breath. "Can't say I've read that one, sir."

I pulled back. This guy was creeping me out.

At that very second, the front door flew open to reveal a large, dark-skinned Indian woman with her arms full. Every single candle in the room blew out.

Chapter 4

TOP TEN REASONS SALEM VILLAGE IS NOT THE "ORLANDO" OF COLONIAL NEW ENGLAND

Ok, I'm going to hurry through this next part, because it's mostly boring. The person who came into the room was named Tituba, an Indian slave that Mr. Parris bought long before he came to Salem. Her job was to keep the Parris household running smoothly, but I didn't really get to know her until later. I've got one word for you here: Voodoo. I also met Betty, the Parris' skinny nine-year old daughter and her eleven-year old cousin, Abigail Williams, who was an orphan the Parris family had taken in. Both of these girls were kind of creepy and let me just say right now for the record, I wish I had never met either of them.

It turned out Reverend Parris was right. I wasn't going to be staying with them. I can't tell you how sad I was about leaving that unhappy place. Boo hoo. After the doctor looked me over (everything was ok except my knee), they farmed me out to some church members named the Proctors. The Proctors owned a huge estate and John Proctor also ran a tavern on the same property. Mr. Procter was this big, older guy around sixty or something, but he was a lot of fun and always told you exactly what was on his mind. I went to live on the farm with John Proctor and his wife, Elizabeth and their kids. My job was to help their servant, Mary Warren. There was a lot to do, so I was pretty much busy from the time I got up in the morning until I collapsed in bed at night. Nothing too exciting happened the first month I was there, but here are some amazing facts that I learned about the hard life of the people of Salem Village that I know you are just dying to find out. Maybe "dying" isn't the best word.

1. NO UNDERWEAR! That's right, you heard me. No underwear. Here's the deal-ee-o. Cloth and clothing in Salem were at a premium. There just wasn't very much of it around. When they needed clothes they couldn't just run down to the local discount store and buy what they wanted. They had to make all of their clothes. You may be thinking that isn't really too bad, but what you don't know is that we had to make the cloth also. In fact most girls my age spent a lot of their time sitting at a spinning wheel making threads out of wool or flax. This was both a complicated and a boring process in which you had to stand up and feed the wool into the spindle and then walk backwards a few feet to draw out the yarn. The finished yarn was then put onto a loom and cloth could be made out of it. It took me a while to get the hang of it, but I finally got it down. When there wasn't anything else to do, all girls put in their time at the spinning wheel. Death by boredom.

So, since cloth was so hard to come by, most people had only a few clothes and I guess underwear was a luxury. When I found out this disgusting fact, I kept a close eye on the pair I was wearing and my long johns. I wasn't giving up my one last remnant of modern society. Now you'll probably want to know about Colonial bathrooms and toilet paper. Surprise, surprise. Neither of them existed. That's right. When you had to go, it was you, the nearest tree or bush and some leaves if you were lucky. Personal hygiene in Salem was not a big priority.

2. IT WAS VERY, VERY, VERY COLD. You can add a few more "very's" in there if you want. The cold was everywhere. You could never escape from it. It wasn't that it was just freezing outside, but it was also very cold inside as well. Yes we had a fireplace, but none of the buildings were insulated and there were huge gaps between windows (few and far between), doors and anywhere two boards came together. You could almost see the cold blowing in. In fact the houses were so drafty you might be standing next to the fire with your face practically burning off and your backside would be popsicle cold. One time I left a cup of water on the fireplace mantle overnight and the next morning it was frozen solid even though the fire blazed all night long.

Because it was bitterly cold, the fireplaces were humongous to provide as much heat as possible. The people of Salem tried to keep as much heat in the house, so the chimneys were small and the inside of any building was very smokey. Unfortunately these hearths were also wide open and occasionally burning pieces of firewood rolled out onto the floor. One of my other jobs was to get these flaming babies back into the fire, before they burned the house down. Another huge problem is that smaller kids were constantly falling into the fireplaces, because they were trying to get close enough to stay warm. I managed to keep a couple of Proctor boys from becoming crispy critters by keeping a sharp eye out.

When it wasn't snowing it was still cold and grey. I didn't think that New England winter in Salem was ever going to end.

3. INDIANS. The villagers of Salem were deathly afraid of Indian attacks with good reason. We were nine miles from Salem Town and were essentially on the frontier. All of those wonderful Thanksgiving stories about the Pilgrims and Squanto were long gone. It didn't take the Indians long to figure out that all the white men wanted to do was steal their land and move them someplace else. The threat of Indian attack was constant. There were many, many people who lived in Salem who had either been the victim of recent Indian attacks in Maine and New Hampshire or had a family member murdered or kidnapped by Indians. Most kidnapping victims were never seen or heard from again. Those who did survive told horrific tales of torture and abuse.

Everywhere you went, everyday, Salem folk had Indian attacks and ambushes on their minds. These random attacks came without any warning and kept everyone just a little bit edgy. Maybe that was part of Reverend Parris' problem. John Proctor didn't seem as worried about it, but he got deathly serious when the frequent subject of Indians came up. I never joked about Indian attacks.

4. WOLVES. As if the Indian problem wasn't bad enough, the Puritans also had to watch out for the roving packs of wolves that dominated the New England landscape. Not only would the wolves attack you out in the wild, some of them were so brazen they

had got into the habit of attacking people and animals in the village. Because their food supply was very limited in the winter, the wolves were especially dangerous this time of year. Oh, really?

Since I had survived the wolf attack, I became a minor celebrity in Salem Village. Everywhere I went, people always wanted to hear my wolf story. Ok, if you give me a dollar. What's a dollar? Never mind. They especially wanted to know how I escaped. I would have told them, if I only knew. I'm certain it made them suspicious when I told them I couldn't remember. Pretty soon it was clear that the Salem-ites were starting to avoid "Limping Wolf Girl."

5. BATHING. This never happened as far as I could tell in Salem Village. I never saw anyone jump in a pond, river or stream. Of course, most of them were frozen. I also never saw anyone wash up for dinner, give themselves a sponge bath or even wash their face when they got up in the morning. Combining this with the fact, that they didn't wash their clothes or linens very often - well you get the picture. Usually you could smell someone coming long before you could see them. Now I'm not crazy about taking a shower every ten minutes, but after a couple of weeks, even I started feeling a little disgusting. I found a cloth and used it to wash up every day or so, but I doubt if it did much good. Since most people avoided me, I guess it didn't make any difference. "Limping Stinky Wolf Girl."

6. CHURCH. This was the "biggie" for the residents of Salem. Most of them were Puritans and attended church on a regular basis. As a servant in the Proctor household I was also required to go to church, even though Mr. Proctor rarely attended. Though this was fundamentally unfair, at least it was better than spinning wool. The church at Salem was very different than any other church I had visited. The men and women came in through separate entrances and sat on opposite sides. There was no singing or hymns or music of any sort. Women were not allowed to speak in church and there were no backs on the wooden benches where we sat. Services mostly consisted of sour Reverend Parris ranting and raving about the Devil and evil and witches. All of the services were simple, long and boring. All of the adult members of the

church referred to each other as "Goody" for the women and "Goodman" for the men. Kind of like you might call someone Mr. or Mrs. Since it was December and the Puritans were so big on church, I was starting to get excited about Christmas until I found out that they didn't observe any religious holidays. You have got to be kidding me.

I did learn by attending church that there was a big dispute in Salem Village about Reverend Parris. I found out that about half the people in town didn't like him and wanted to get rid of him. You could put me on this list. As a result of this he hadn't been paid for about two years and a lot of people had stopped going to church. No wonder he was so cranky.

7. TOOTHBRUSHES. Don't ask. Same goes for deodorant, body soap, shampoo, etc. Of course most of the people in Salem Village were limited to three or four teeth.

8. EDUCATION. Life in Salem was amazingly hard. Everyone in each household was busy doing something just to survive. They were either spinning wool, making butter or cheese, sewing clothes, preparing food, taking care of children, hunting, making candles, tending to the animals, going to church, farming, watching out for Indians and wolves or one of the other million things that needed to be done. There was no place to go shopping, so everything that we used had to be made, traded or grown. The only time for education was in the evening after the work was done, so there were no schools.

The education that children received was done at home, by their parents. Much of it was religious in nature. John and Elizabeth Proctor were amazed that I knew how to read so well, so one of my new jobs was to help educate their sons. I was dying to tell those boys about skateboards and video games, but I kept my mouth shut. I still didn't know who I could trust in Salem Village.

9. FUN. As you can tell the Puritans weren't too big on frivolity. Even though everybody was deathly serious, every once in awhile they would get together and play some games. Someone

might even break out a fiddle and everyone would clap and sing. Big whoop. I heard that some of the girls hung out on Sunday nights at the Parris house for a little fun. Mr. Proctor wasn't too keen on letting me go over there, but I was about to go crazy with all of the hard work and only the boys for company. Even though the Parris house was full of strange people, I was desperate to make some friends.

10. FOOD. In the winter there were almost no fruits or vegetables. Mostly we had milk, butter and cheese from the cows and goats, eggs, bread, porridge, wild game that the men hunted and once in awhile a slaughtered pig or a goose from the yard. Woohoo! Sugar and salt were rare, so everything had almost little or no flavor. I was working my fingers to the bone though, so by the time a meal rolled around I was always ready to chow down. No questions asked. In conclusion, as you probably noticed life in Salem Village was incredibly difficult at best. It was miserably cold, overcast, gloomy, smoky, smelly, and full of dissension, mistrust and fear. Fear of your neighbors, fear of Indians, fear of wolves and most of all fear of the Devil. It was one endless, desperate cycle: days upon days of fear, hard work and bad weather. In short, Salem Village was the perfect place for something terrible to happen.

Chapter 5
WHODOO VOODOO?

Title: Maddie's Very Large Mouth - A Play in Three Scenes

Scene I - The Proctor Home

The setting: January, 1692, Salem Village. It is a cold, grey Sunday afternoon. Inside the two-story Proctor home everyone is quietly enjoying the blazing fire. Goody Proctor is knitting, the Proctor boys are playing something on the floor and John Proctor is dozing in a chair with his feet propped up. The two servant girls, Maddie and Mary are nowhere to be seen.

Maddie enters. (stage right)
Maddie: Uh, Mr. Proctor: (she shakes him.)
Proctor: Ummmmm. (she shakes him, again, this time more forcefully). What, what is it? (sleepily)
Maddie: Have you been thinking about it?
Proctor: About what? (he wipes his massive hands across his face and yawns)
Maddie: Letting me go. (exasperated).
Proctor: You will be the death of me, child (irritated).
Maddie: Well? (Pleading).
Proctor: You know I don't like those people. Parris seems more like a man of this world with his constant complaining about salary and firewood, than a man of God.
Maddie: You promised!
Proctor: Well, I never.
Maddie: Ok, you almost promised.
Goodie Proctor: John, for goodness sake, let the child go. She's been working her fingers to the bone around here. She deserves a little time with girls of her own age. Try to remember when you were a young man.
Proctor: Hrrrummppph. Grunt.
Goodie Proctor: I think that means you can go, Maddie.

31

Maddie: Really? (excitedly)

Proctor: Take Mary Warren with you and be home by nine. If you're late, you won't ever be goin' again. And be careful, there's devils in those woods. (laughing).

A few minutes later Maddie and Mary leave though the front door. (Stage left). A light snow blows into the room as they leave.

Scene Two - The Parris' Kitchen

The setting: The kitchen is crowded with girls, some of them still children, some teenagers. Tituba, the Parris' Indian slave is in the middle of the group, standing up and waving her arms excitedly. Around her, sitting on the floor are seven girls: Betty Parris, Abigail Williams, Mary Warren, Maddie, Ann Putnam (the 12 year old daughter of the influential and powerful Putnam family), Mercy Lewis (the Putnam's 17 year old servant who had witnessed both of her parents murdered by Indians) Mary Walcott (Ann Putnam's 18 year old cousin and best friend) and , Elizabeth Hubbard. (17 year old servant of Dr. Griggs). The mood is one of giddy excitement.

Ann: Tell us another story, Tituba, about Barbados. Tell us one full of voodoo and witchcraft.

Betty: Please, please, please!

Abigail: Tell us about the Black Man and his book.

Tituba: You girls know dem stories too scary for you. You be havin' nightmares. Sides, you know Reverend Parris beat me for telling you dem stories.

Several girls: We won't tell! We won't tell!

Maddie (aside, sotto voce) These gals need to get a life. Oh yeah, I forgot. No one in Salem has one.

Tituba: Well this be a true story, but you better not be a repeatin' it. I was walkin' down the road jus' the other night, and de moon was full as, as full as a tick fat with blood, (Maddie rolls her eyes), and den dis big black dog jumped out at me all snarling and slobbering...

Abigail: Go on, go on.

Ann: Tell us, tell us and don't leave anything out.

Tituba: Den he says to me in a terrible booming voice, "SERVE ME".

Someone screams.

Reverend Parris rushes in. (stage left)

Parris: What's going on in here? Tituba? (He looks into the scared faces of the girls.) Tituba, I have warned you repeatedly about frightening these girls with your wicked stories..
Betty: Father, she wasn't. That was me who screamed when I accidently spilled some hot tea on my leg.
Maddie: (mouthing to the audience) Liar.
Parris: All right then. You girls quiet down, now. I am preparing next week's sermon and I need to concentrate. Tituba, I have warned you for the last time. Heed my warning.
Tituba: Yes, Master.

Reverend Parris exits slowly, stremly looking back. (stage left)
Several girls: Go on, go on now, Tituba.

Tituba: (whispering now) Den de dog he turned into..., into... a man. He had a yellow bird with him which kept pecking at de bloody spot on his hand, and red cat and a black cat...
Maddie: (aside, sotto voce) This could be the lamest story I've ever heard. The headless horseman is about fifty times better.
Tituba: (continuing) den he gets up right aside me and ask me..., ask me...
Ann: What, what, what is it?
Tituba: (eyes widening) ...to sign his book with my...blood.
Several girls: Gasping.
Silence.
Tituba jumps and turns in the air grasping at the girls frightening them.
Tituba: Den we all fly into de black night and put spells on all of you. Then we fly to Barbados to get out of dis miserable cold. HA, HA, HA, HA, A HA, HA, HA, HA! (doubled over with laughter)
Abigail: Tituba, you are so mean.
Ann: That's not funny.
Maddie: Yes it was. Good one, Tituba.

Ann: (glaring) Maybe Maddie can tell us how she "flew" here after the wolves attacked her. Maybe she flew to our house with Tituba. What about it, Maddie?

Tituba: Yeah, me and Maddie been flying all around telling dem boys not to marry you.

Abigail: Oh, Tituba. How about some fortune telling? Tell us about our future husbands.

Betty: No, lets make poppets and torture crazy Goody Good. (standing up and pretending to be Good). Oh, please, please give me some food to eat. I'm sooooo hungry and soooo poor. What, no food?! You cursed, wretched children...

Ann: (laughing) No, no, I know. Let's torture Goody Osborn instead. I'm old and I'm rich, so I can marry my servant...

Abigail: No, no, no. Tell me who I'm going to marry, Tituba.

Tituba: Betty, go and get me a glass of water.

Betty goes to a cabinet and gets out a glass. She ladles it full with water. The girls hover around the table and Tituba produces an egg. She slowly holds it up for everyone to see.

Maddie: What's this all about?

Abigail: Don't be silly, wolf-girl. The egg white will tell us who our future husbands will be. It's like a crystal ball.

Maddie: Can't say that I've ever heard of that one before.

Ann: (hissing) Sssshhhh. No one cares what you've heard of.

Betty: Me first, me first.

Tituba: Quietly now. (she puts a finger to her lips and then gingerly holds the egg above the glass)

She gently cracks the egg and carefully drops only the white into the glass. The room is deathly silent, except for a distant crackling fire. The girls stare intently into the glass.

Betty: What...what is it? Tituba, what does it say?

Tituba: Wait.. wait...wait.

Ann: Oh my goodness!

Abigail: (whispering) It looks like...it looks like...a like a some kind of box.

Ann: It's not a box,... it's a coffin.

Silence. Tituba gasps and leaves the room. (Exit stage right).

Ann: Congratulations, Betty. Your husband is going to be Tituba's bird man. You are going to marry the Devil.
Betty: (almost crying) That's not funny, Ann.
Ann: I'm not funning you. You are a bride of death.
Abigail: Stop it, Ann. Stop it right now.
Ann: Suit yourself. I know what I saw.
Maddie: (changing the subject). Hey, guess what, guys. I can't predict the future, but I can tell you exactly what it's going to be like.
Ann: Oh, really.
Maddie: (aside) Ok, I got them now. I'm going to blow their little Colonial minds.
Maddie: Sure did you know that in the future everyone is going to be able to talk to each other from far, far away? You won't need horses to ride, because we'll all be riding around in shiny metal boxes. You'll be able to get from Salem to Boston in about a half an hour.
Abigail: Maddie, you're just trying to impress us.
Maddie: No, no. It's all true. We're all going to be able to fly around in gigantic silver tubes with wings. You will be able to listen to any music anytime you want, just by putting tiny little earpieces in your ears. (rolling now).
Betty: Really?
Maddie: That's just the beginning. You will be able to have heat and light anytime you want it.

Maddie goes on for several minutes explaining the marvels of modern civilization and all the girls are transfixed on her as she speaks. Finally Mary Warren interrupts.

Mary: Uh, Maddie, I think we should be getting home now.
Maddie: But I have lots more to tell them. I could go on for hours.
Mary: Oh, I think you've said quite enough.

Maddie and Mary get their cloaks and hats on and prepare to leave.
Ann: Maddie, you can come back anytime. We REALLY like your stories. (laughing)

35

Maddie and Mary exit stage left.

Scene Three: A dark road in the Salem Village. The girls hurry home as snow continues to fall.

Maddie: Hey, Mary. How come we had to leave so soon? I was just warming up.
Mary: Maddie, I don't know where you got all those stories, but they are only going to get you into trouble.
Maddie: What are you talking about. I was only having a little fun for once.
Mary: Maddie, don't you know about those girls?
Maddie: What do you mean?
Mary: Ann Putnam is the meanest girl in town and Betty Parris and Abigail Williams aren't much better. I stay as far away from them as I possibly can. Whatever you do, don't tell Mr. Proctor what happened tonight. He will never let us out of the house again.

Maddie frowns. A wolf howls in the distance. A cloud covers the moon and the girls run home as the curtain falls.

Chapter 6

DOUBLE, DOUBLE TOIL AND TROUBLE
FIRE BURN, AND CAULDRON BUBBLE

I didn't sleep very well that night, and the next morning I remembered what Mary had said about not telling Mr. Proctor about the little get-together. Just in case I had forgotten, Mary shot me a look that would have melted an icicle. It was hard not talking to Mr. Proctor though. He was a lot of fun and sometimes it seemed like he was the only one who had any sense. I kept my head down and my mouth shut for the next couple of days, but one night after supper I cornered him while he was getting firewood.

"Hey, Mr. Proctor. Can I ask you something?"
"It depends."
"On what?"
"How much of this wood you're going to help me carry."
"I'm serious."
"So am I."

He piled up some wood onto my open arms, and I followed him inside.

"Alright, what is it?"
"Mr. Proctor, what do you think of all these people around here talking about devils, witches and spirits and stuff."

He stroked his beard.

"Well, Maddie, the Devil's real enough, but I'm pretty certain he don't need no agents flying around helping him. There's evil enough in this world without all that other nonsense."

"Is that why you never go to church with us?"

"No, the reason that I don't go to church is because I don't trust that Parris fellow. All he ever seems to worry about is his salary and how much wood we owe him. Half the people in that congregation are more worried about their property than they are their own souls. Take that Putnam for instance. He has quarrels and land disputes with just about everyone around here. I won't sit in the same church with such a man."

I paused for a minute.

"Mr. Proctor, do you know Goody Good."
"Sarah? Of course. Why?"
"Do you think there's something wrong with her? I'm mean, what's up with her?"

"Nothing a little money or property wouldn't fix. She just a poor woman who's had a string of bad fortune. She's homeless. Destitute really. She used to have property, but she had to sell it to pay her debts. Now she's reduced to begging for food and work. We try to help her out as much as we can."

"You don't think, you don't think she's..."
"She's what? Spit it out."
"She's a...a...witch?"

I could barely say the word. John Proctor looked at me with shock and amazement.

"Why Maddie, who has filled your head with such evil silliness? Goody Good is no more of witch than I am."

His eyes narrowed and he stared at me long and hard.

"Maddie, does this have anything at all to do with your visit to the Parris house a few days ago? I knew nothing good would come of you spending time with those spiteful, wicked children."

He grabbed me by the wrist.

"Tell me child, what happened that night."

I pulled away.

"Nothing..., Mr. Proctor,... nothing. I swear it."

I ran to the room I shared with Mary, but I knew that he knew that I was lying.

I missed the next service at church because I wasn't feeling well, but the following Sunday Ann Putnam kept trying to get my attention. I did everything I could to avoid her. I didn't see Betty Parris or Abigail Williams that day, but Reverend Parris seemed more agitated and upset than usual. Just as I was about to leave after the service, Ann caught me by my cloak and jerked me aside. Her eyes were bright.

"Maddie, have you heard? Have you heard about Betty Parris? Have you, have you?"

She was practically licking her lips she was so excited. I tried to pull away, but she held me tight with both hands.

"No, I haven't heard, and I don't want to hear. I don't want to know anything about you and your weird-o friends. Now leave me alone."

"Oh, Maddie, it's not quite that easy. You were there that night. You witnessed what happened."

"Nothing happened. It was just a stupid game."

"Then why is Betty forgetting her errands and barking like a dog?"

"What?!"

"That's right, you heard me. Betty's been sobbing and throwing Bibles and saying that she is damned..."

"Stop it, stop it, stop it you stupid moron. You're just trying to stir up trouble. Let me go."

I finally tore away from her and covered my ears. I could still hear her laughter ringing in my head as I hurried to the Proctor's. Now more than ever I just wanted to find a way to get home and away from this creepy place. Far, far away.

The next week I tried to keep to my business and stay out of trouble, but Salem Village was full of rumors about Betty Parris and now Abigail Williams. I heard someone say they found the girls hiding under chairs and making odd gestures and faces. They were talking gibberish that no one could understand. This was just crazy.

By the end of February, Salem Village was in complete turmoil. Betty and Abigail were not any better and Dr. Griggs had been summoned to examine them. Dr Griggs said they were under an evil hand, and the rumors were flying that the girls were bewitched. Reverend Parris was getting advice from other ministers in surrounding towns. They tried several home remedies to cure the girls, but nothing worked. I think all they needed was a good spanking.

John Proctor was getting more and more frustrated and forbade me to attend church or have anything to do with the Parris household. He didn't have to tell me twice. Would this cold, dark, depressing winter ever end? Not anytime soon.

On Friday, February 26th, 1692 things went from bad to worse. When I came in that evening after doing my chores I saw John and Goody Proctor huddling in the corner talking quietly. They both looked frightened and stopped talking when I entered the room. After dinner, Mary and I were sent to bed early. Just like me, Mary had only heard rumors and didn't know if anything new had taken place. After she fell asleep, I slipped out of bed and tiptoed to the door. I gently pushed it open just a crack, so I could hear the Proctors talking.

"Oh, Elizabeth, this is the biggest bunch of horse manure I have ever heard."

"Calm down, John, and listen to what I am trying to tell you."

"I absolutely refuse to be calm."

"Do you know about the witch cake?"

"The what?"

"It came out today that yesterday when the Parris' were out of town, Tituba made a witch cake..."

"What in the world?..."

"Stop interrupting me, John, and I will tell you. She made a cake out of rye meal and mixed it with Betty and Abigail's urine..."

Stop the presses. Did I hear this right? They made a cupcake out of rye and pee?

"...and then they fed it to the dog..."

Now I'm going to throw up.

"...to see if the dog showed any of the same symptoms as the afflicted and to break the spell."

Mr. Proctor was roaring now.

"They are inviting disaster..."

"Quiet now, John. Listen...listen. This only made the girls worse and when the Parris' returned, the girls told them about the witch-cake, and then they accused Tituba of being a witch."

"And then?"

"I only heard that the Reverend Parris called several neighboring ministers and gentlemen of Salem to observe the girls."

"Observe them doing what?"

"They say their bodies are twisted and contorted into grotesque shapes and that they are tormented..."

"Tormented by what?"

"Tormented by invisible apparitions."

This was just unbelievable. In fact, I didn't believe it. Those girls were up to something. The last thing I saw that night was John Proctor holding his massive head in his hands. That image kept me awake for a long, long time. Despite Mr. Proctor's warnings, I was going to have to find out for myself what in the devil was going on.

Chapter 7
WITCH HUNT

I had another night of restless sleep. Even when I finally dozed off, I kept having weird nightmares about talking cats and human-headed birds flying everywhere and trying to peck at me. The next day was Saturday, and I got up at daylight and finished my chores early. Then without asking I slipped away into a howling wind. I doubted Mr. Proctor would be too excited about me going into town today.

Salem Village was in full-blown panic mode. Everyone was running from place to place or huddling from the cold in small, whispering groups. No one had a smile on their face or a kind word to say to me. I tried not to make eye contact and hurried as quickly as I could to the Putnam house. My plan was to confront Ann and put a stop to this nonsense once and for all. I couldn't wait to tell her what I thought of all this foolishness.

When I reached the Putnam's I was shocked by what I saw. The front yard of the Putnam house was overflowing with all of the people of Salem Village. There was plenty of arguing and I saw John and Goody Proctor huddled with another group of people talking. Mr. Proctor was gesturing wildly. I slipped around the side of the house to avoid them and grabbed the first woman who walked by.

"Hey, what's going on? What's all the excitement about?"
"Haven't you heard?"
"Heard what?"
"Ann Putnam's afflicted too. She's accused Tituba of trying to kill her and the other girls."

I gasped and must have turned white as a sheet. My knees buckled.
"Are you all right, child?"

43

"Uh, yes...yes, I'm fine."

I struggled to gain my composure. The last thing I wanted was to draw attention to myself.

"Where is Ann?"
"She's inside with her parents and Reverend Parris."
"Parris?"
"Yes, but he probably won't be there for long."

She turned and pulled away, walking. I called after her.

"Why not?"

"Dr. Grigg's niece, Elizabeth Hubbard, is also having fits and attacks. She said a wolf was stalking her, and she's accused Goody Good and Goody Osborn of being witches and tormenting her."

"What do they do with witches around here?"

She looked back at me strangely.
"Why, they hang them, of course."

I stood silent in the blowing wind and snow. I was numb, but not from the cold. This situation was snowballing out of control. I knew those girls would enjoy all the attention they were about to be getting. No one in Salem society paid any attention to girls my age. We were practically invisible. We were simply uneducated workers waiting to grow a little older just to become someone's wife. We had no voice, no control, no hope and no future. Now just a little winter fun game had turned into something extremely dangerous and powerful.

I hadn't forgot my failed attempts to change the past, but I just couldn't stand by and let these terrible things happen. There was only one person who could stop all this. Tituba. Tituba could tell all the adults we were just fooling around and trying to have

44

some fun on a cold winter night. I shook the snow off my shoulders, stamped my feet and headed off to the Parris house.

It didn't surprise me to see yet another crowd in front of the Parris'. The whole town was in an uproar. I crept around to the back hoping to sneak in and talk with Tituba, before it was too late. When I turned the corner I saw Tituba curled up in a pathetic ball near the woodpile. She was sobbing uncontrollably. I gently touched her shoulder.

"No more, no more! ...Why, who you be? Who goes dere?"

"I'm Maddie, remember, Tituba. I was at your house when you were telling stories and playing those silly games." I wiped her face with the back of my hand.

She just shook her head, slowly and sadly.

"Tituba, what is it? Why are you crying?"
"He beat me, Maddie. He beat it out of me. I be saying it wasn't true, but he jus' kept a hittin' me."

"Who, what?"
"Parris. He jus' kept comin' at me like a crazy man."
"Oh, Tituba. Are you all right? What did you tell him?"

She looked at me, her eyes wide with fear.
"Oh, Maddie. I didn' have no choice. I couldn' hold up no more."

"What, Tituba, what is it? What did you tell that evil man?"

A group of angry men came storming around the corner before she could answer.
"There she is! Get her! Don't let her escape."

Tituba screamed and tried to get up and run. Someone shoved me to the ground, and then they quickly surrounded her. I saw Parris and Putnam in that wild circle, their faces flushed with excitement.

"Seize the witch! SEIZE HER!"

I instantly decided there was nothing I could do to stop them, and quietly receded into the shadows of a barn nearby. The last thing I saw was Tituba collapsing like a rag doll into the arms of her accusers, her mournful wail echoing around me in the still, frozen woods. I quietly slunk back through those woods, keeping a sharp eye out for that wolf. I didn't say a peep to the Proctors that night and they didn't say anything to me either. We ate our supper in complete silence and went to bed.

When I woke up the next morning, Sunday, February 28th, the wind was howling, cracking and whipping through the deserted streets of Salem. As the day went by the storms intensified. No one even bothered to go outside. This was the absolute worse weather of the entire winter. The wind blew, rain slashed and the already full rivers flooded, washing away bridges and buildings. The roads were impassable. I shivered all day long. It was as if both natural and supernatural forces had descended on Salem Village wreaking physical and spiritual destruction. I wanted to talk to Mr. Proctor about what was happening, but the words simply escaped me.

The next day, Thomas Putnam, Ann's father, swore out complaints before the magistrates charging Tituba. Sarah Good, and Sarah Osborn with suspicion of witchcraft. By Tuesday morning, all three were in custody and being held at Ingersoll's tavern. When news of the arrests spread, the Village of Salem was flooded again, this time with people. The weather had cleared and the bad roads did little to prevent people from coming into town to see the spectacle. When the magistrates finally got to Salem Village, the proceedings had to be moved to a bigger meeting house because of the crowds. Even though I was supposed to be working, I managed to ease into the meeting house and find an inconspicuous place to watch the questioning. I didn't see the Proctors, but I still didn't want to draw any unwanted attention.

All three of the accused were to appear before the court, one at a time. Betty Parris, Abigail Williams, Ann Putnam and Elizabeth Hubbard, their accusers, were fidgeting and twisting, off to the side. I swear I saw Ann Putnam smirking. I tried to get a good look into her eyes, but I was too far away. The constable brought in Sarah Good and you could have heard a pin drop. I had seen Sarah Good around the village, but had never spoken with her. The judge began to question her.

"What evil spirits have you brought to harm these children?"

"None."

"Did you make a contract with the Devil? Did you sign his book?"

"No."

"Why do you hurt these children?"
"I have never hurt them."

These kinds of questions went on for several minutes, but Goody Good continued to deny the charges. The judge asked the girls to confirm their accusations. All four of them twisted and turned and pulled back in fear from the accused. They said Goody Good's spirit lunged at them.

Oh, brother.

Goody Good never admitted the accusations, but she did say it might be one of the other accused who was torturing the girls. The magistrates were not convinced and ordered Sarah Good to stand trial for being a witch.

The next one they brought out was Sarah Osborn, who seemed even more bewildered than Sarah Good. I had never seen Goody Osborn, because she was old and sickly and never left the house. After the girls accused her, seeming visibly hurt by her, the magistrate coldly stared her down.

"What is your relationship with Sarah Good?"

"None. I have not seen her for the past two years."

"Sarah Good says that it was you who have harmed the children."

"I don't know that the Devil goes around in my likeness to do anyone harm."

"Why haven't you been going to church?"

"I have been too sick to go. I almost never leave my house. I have been ill for the past fourteen months."

Despite her denials and her ill health the magistrates also kept her in prison to stand trial.

This would have been funny if it wasn't so sad.

After a brief break for lunch, a disturbed Tituba was led in. I could tell by her face and her posture that she had no will to stand up to her accusers. The girls groaned and twisted and cried out just like when the first two were brought before them. I just wanted to slap them.

After a few minutes of denial, the magistrate honed in.

"Who is it that hurts these children?'
"It's the Devil, for all I know."
"What shape is he like when he hurts them?"

She whispered.
"I saw him yesterday. He was like...like a man. He told me to serve him, but I refused."

The girls seem to relax after Tituba abandoned her innocence.

"So, who have you seen hurting these poor children?"

"Four women."

"Who were they?"

"Two women from Boston and...and...Goody Osborn and Sarah Good."

Someone in the crowd gasped and there was murmuring all around me.

"They came up from Boston with a tall man and threatened to hurt me if I did not hurt the children. At first I agreed and then I changed my mind."

Tituba's testimony just grew more shocking and increasingly bizarre. She seemed to admit anything they suggested to her. She talked about spirits appearing to her in the form of hogs and great black dogs and yellow birds and black and red cats. She probably would have said pink elephants if someone mentioned them. All these "spirits" told her to pinch and hurt the girls. She went on to say that Sara Good and Osborn had told her to murder Ann Putnam with a knife. The questions went on and on, and Tituba dug herself in deeper and deeper.

The girls started acting crazy again and the magistrate asked Tituba who hurt them.

"It is Goody Good. She hurts them with her shape."

I just shook my head back and forth slowly. It should have been clear to anyone watching that Tituba had no idea of what she was saying. I couldn't believe she didn't mention the beating Reverend Parris gave her. I gradually realized there was nothing I could do to help any of these poor women. No one was going to believe a twelve year old orphaned servant girl, who didn't even know where she came from. I silently slipped out from the proceedings. I didn't care about the weather, the Indians or the wolves. This place had gone absolutely crazy. Someway, somehow, I had to get out of Salem Village as fast as I could.

Chapter 8

EXIT SALEM

The next day I began hoarding food and plotting my escape from Salem Village. I knew from my previous journeys that I couldn't just strike out in the dead of winter. What I needed was a plan. Because of the bad weather and the bad roads there was no way I could leave right away. It wasn't that far to Boston, but my chances for survival increased dramatically if I could hang on until the weather broke, and it got a little warmer. If I had enough food and the weather and roads were half decent, then the only things I had to worry about were the Indians and the wolves. No problem. Oh yeah, I forgot about these "witch addled" Puritans. They would probably track me all the way to Boston, if they thought I was part of this insanity.

I almost confided in Mary to see if she could help me, but I finally decided that I was going to have to go it alone. Somehow John Proctor had found out that Mary had attended the first court appearances, and he was absolutely livid. He threatened to beat us both senseless if he found out that either of us were participating in any way with these trials. After that, I was afraid to tell him where I had been or mention anything at all about what was going on in the village. If I said anything to Mary about my plan, she might tell Mr. Proctor, and there was no telling what he would do. I just couldn't risk it.

I had absolutely no problem heeding Mr. Proctor's warnings about staying away from what was going on in town. I stopped going to church, and stayed as close to home as possible. Even though I was determined to mind my own business, the bad news about the terrible events unfolding kept finding me. It seemed like every day there was some new shocking revelation coming from the "afflicted". Mary seemed to be more and more troubled about what was going on around us. She was good friends with Elizabeth Hubbard (one of the accusers), and I was constantly afraid she was going to spill the beans about what had happened the night we visited Tituba.

First, I heard that Reverend Parris had sent his daughter Betty to live with a distant relative. Next I heard that Elizabeth Hubbard and Abigail Williams accused two other women in Salem Village of tormenting them. I didn't know Martha Corey or Rebecca Nurse, but I overheard John Proctor tell his wife that Rebecca Nurse was seventy years old and frail and sickly. I think that his exact comment was that if Goody Nurse were a witch, then everybody was.

The most disturbing news of all came a few days later. I couldn't believe my ears when I found out that Ann Putnam, Sr. had joined the ranks of the accusers. That's right, now it wasn't only children and teenage girls having the fits and absurd behavior. Now the girls had been joined by several other full grown women who claimed to be tormented by specters and witches. Of course with Ann Putnam, Jr. and Mercy Lewis, her servant, both spending all day being tormented and testifying, Ann Putnam, Sr. was stuck doing all of the chores and taking care of her five children. You'd probably feel like you were being attacked to, with all that work to do. Actually this wasn't funny. With adults joining the children this mess wasn't going to end anytime soon. That troubling news only increased my resolve to get the heck out of Salem Village.

Around April it finally started warming up a little. I had plenty of food and a pretty good idea of where I needed to go. Most of the roads had dried out and some of the bridges had been repaired. I wasn't really certain how I was going to deal with the wolves and the Indians, but my basic idea was to stay on the road during the daytime and to try and find farmhouses or barns to stay in at night. I knew it wouldn't be safe to travel at night. I thought about saying goodbye to everyone, but I figured it would just raise suspicions about me. Besides I knew that Mary Warren had been sneaking into town for the hearings and her behavior was getting more bizarre. I saw Mr. Proctor shake her fiercely one night and warn her about going into town. She spent the next couple of days at the spinning wheel and that seemed to calm her down a little. I was going to miss the Proctor boys, but I just had to get out of Salem.

I set out for Boston early, Monday, April 11, 1692. I had to go back through town to get on the road to Boston. I didn't have a map, but I suspected I could follow the traffic most of the way. I was just about all the way out of town when a breathless Mary Warren spun me around in the middle of the road.

> "Maddie, Maddie, please stop!" Her eyes were wide with fear. "You CAN'T leave me."

> "Mary, let me go. I can't stay. This place is just a little bit wacko for my taste. Let go of my arm, please. Now."

> "Maddie, if you leave I will tell them everything that happened that night."

> "I don't care, Mary. I've got to get out of this evil place."

Mary fell on the ground and starting writhing around like she had ants in her pants.

> "Maddie, stop pinching me. Please, stop."

What? I was standing about five feet from her. Fortunately there was no one else around.

She was bigger than me, but I had the advantage of being just about as mad as I've ever been. I grabbed her by her cloak and dragged her up to her knees.

> "Mary, you have got to STOP this foolishness. We are both going to end up in prison or worse. Don't you get it? This is only going to come back to haunt us. You have got to get control of yourself. If you want to go with me, you can, but I am not staying in Salem another second."
> "Maddie, Maddie, you cannot go."

She desperately held on to my skirt, sobbing and shrieking as I dragged her for a few feet down the road. I gave her a swift kick and finally broke free. She was nearly hysterical. I marched down the road without looking back.

"MADDIE! They've taken Elizabeth Proctor!"

I did a slow turn, and saw Mary Warren collapsed in a heap in the middle of the road. Her tear stained face looked up at me in utter despair.

"Say... that... again."
"Oh, Maddie, what will we ever do? This morning they took Goody Proctor into custody. She...is...accused."

This news took my breath away. I stood there in disbelief. I had lived with the Proctors now for about four months. The Proctors didn't have the happiest home in the world, but who would ever think Goody Proctor could be a witch? Did John Proctor know? He was going to go absolutely bananas. Who would take care of the boys? My mind started going a million miles a minute. Wait a minute. This wasn't my problem. I was leaving Salem Village for good. Wasn't I?

"When is she to be examined?"

I bent over and shook her.

"Mary, listen to me! When is she going before the court?"

"Today...today."

She was drained from her emotional outburst.
"The Governor's Council will attend her trial this morning."

I dragged Mary up to her feet, and I propped her up as we straggled back toward Salem Village. I couldn't believe I was actually going back there. I must have been losing my mind. I just couldn't let the only man in Salem Village who had been kind to me go through this alone. I had to tell him what I thought was going on. As we made our way back to the village, I tried not to imagine how angry and upset he must be.

When we got to the meeting house, it was jammed packed just like the last time I had been there. I sent Mary home to tend to the boys, and then I managed to squeeze in through a side door. Tituba's husband, John Indian, was testifying. Elizabeth Hubbard stood with the other accusers, almost in a trance. Mary Walcott convulsed in a series of writhing seizures. Abigail Williams reported she had seen forty witches taking communion with her own blood in her uncle's pasture. John Indian testified Goody Proctor had tortured him. I didn't think it was possible, but the accusers behavior and testimony had actually gotten more unbelievable since the last time I was there.

Finally, Elizabeth Proctor was called. I strained to see John Proctor in the crowd, but my view was partially blocked by a post. He had to be here somewhere. Goody Proctor stood silently and confidently before the council.

"Elizabeth Proctor, do you understand you have been charged with acts of witchcraft? What say you to these charges? How do you answer?"
"I am innocent."

The judge then turned to the accusers.
"Does she hurt you?"

Abigail Williams jammed her whole hand into her mouth. I almost started laughing. The other accusers stood silently.

"Indian John. Does she afflict you?"

"She came and she choked me. She brought me the black book to sign it."

Suddenly I heard John Proctor's deep voice.

55

"Indian John, if I ever see you outside of this court, I will soon beat the Devil out of you."

"Goody Proctor?"

"As God is my witness, I know nothing of these things."

"Ann Putnam, does she hurt you?"

When Goody Proctor turned her icy stare towards Ann, she and the other girls fell onto the ground in convulsions.

"She hurts us and she brings her maid to have us sign the book."

Uh, oh. Just as I had feared, it now looked like Mary Warren was also being accused. Just then Abigail Williams and Ann Putnam put on their best show yet. They writhed and wriggled on the floor, screaming like they were being tormented by demons. Suddenly Abigail stopped and pointed toward the ceiling. As one, the crowd looked up toward where she was pointing.

"There is Goody Proctor! She is up on that beam with her yellow birds!"

Of course, the beams were empty, but that important fact seemed to escape everyone in the room except me.

"She comes with Goodman Proctor to hurt us! Goodman Proctor is a wizard and he is pulling up Mrs. Pope's feet."

Mrs. Pope was one of the new adult accusers. Almost on cue, her feet flew up into the air. Again, most normal people would be laughing by now, but no one in the room seemed to think this was funny.

Suddenly I saw an enraged John Proctor struggle to the front. He was desperately trying to keep his composure. I saw him take a deep breath and his speech was slow and measured. He spoke through clenched teeth.

"Enough! This complete, utter nonsense MUST come to an end. Right here and right now. These silly girls are ruining the lives of innocent citizens like me and my wife, and if this court is foolish enough to believe them, than I condemn you as well."

He pounded his fist for emphasis.

By now the courtroom was a three-ringed circus. With every one of John Proctor's words the accusers fell back in horror. They dropped to the ground convulsing as if they were being attacked and shaken by specters. They screamed and shrieked, calling out that Goodman Proctor was trying to kill them. Abigail Williams and Ann Putnam both tried to hit Elizabeth Proctor in the head with their fists, but were repelled by an unseen force. They then fell to the ground screeching in obvious pain, claiming their fingers were burned. The crowd stared at all of this in dumbfounded amazement. All we needed was some popcorn and cotton candy.

When the magistrates finally got things back under control, one of them ordered that John Proctor be taken into custody and held over for trial. I just couldn't believe this was happening.

"But, Sir! I am innocent!"

John Proctor's booming protest fell on deaf ears. In short order both he and Goody Proctor were escorted out. The proceedings were then closed with prayer. This wild day, the day of my would-be escape from Salem, ended with both of the Proctors in the Salem Village jail waiting to stand trial for witchcraft. And me, I obviously wasn't on my way to Boston. I was back in the last place in the world I wanted to be. I trudged slowly back to the Proctors, but I had no idea what I was going to do next.

Chapter 9
TRIAL AND ERROR

I was certain that Mary had something to do with the fact the Proctors were now in jail accused as witches. I decided not to confront her about it, because she was in such a fragile emotional state. I needed her to help me with the Proctor children until I could figure out what to do. John Proctor's older grown son also came to live with us to help out with the Proctor brood. He wasn't too keen on cooking and cleaning though.

Two things I knew for sure: I knew that the Proctors were not witches and that Mary Warren was seriously disturbed. I figured it was just a matter of time before she was arrested and accused of witchcraft. There's no telling what she would say at that point to save her neck. I still wanted to get out of Salem, but I was torn between my loyalty to the Proctors and my fear of all the accusations flying around. Sooner or later one of those crazy girls was going to point her crooked finger at me. With the exception of the Proctors, most of the people accused so far were women and outsiders on the fringes of Salem society. Just like me.

I needed to talk to Mr. Proctor to find out what he wanted me to do. I was certain that if I could testify at his trial that he would be found innocent. The only problem was that I would have to go back into town and talk to him at the jail. Plus I knew that it wouldn't look good for me to be found talking to one of the accused. I decided the best thing to do was to sneak over to the jail at night and see if I could talk to him without anyone finding out.

It was a chilly, moonless April night as I made my way to the Salem jail. I was so worried about being spotted I actually forgot about the wolves and the Indians for awhile. I kept my head down and well covered. When I got to the jail, I found a barrel and pushed it close to an open window. Standing on my tip-toes on top of the barrel, I could barely reach the sill. I whispered as loud as I could.

"Is John Proctor there?"
"Who goes there?"

I took a big chance.

"It's Maddie. Maddie Tucker. The Proctor's servant girl."

"Maddie, it's me, Goody Proctor. What are you doing here?"

"I need, I need to talk to Mr. Proctor. Where is he?"

"I think he is on the other side. Be careful, child."

I nearly knocked the barrel over getting down. Some crazy dog heard me and started barking. I scurried around to the other side of the building. No barrels, but another window. I went back around to the other side and got the barrel. I started rolling it around, but my knee was killing me. I finally got it under the window, but that darn dog would not shut up. I had to hurry. I scrambled up and held myself up by the windowsill.

"John Proctor. John Proctor. Hey, Mr. Proctor!"

As loud as I could chance it.

"What, what is it? Has some specter come to torment me?"

It was Mr. Proctor.

"Mr. Proctor, it's me Maddie."
"Have you come to set me free?"
"I wish I could, but I need to know what you want me to do?"

Silence. More barking.

"You must stop Mary from accusing us. I don't think they will believe the other girls, but since she lived with us they may believe her."

Just then someone came around the side of the building, and I fell off the barrel. Thud. Must have been that stupid dog that tipped them off. I managed to get away without them seeing me, but they had to be blind to see that I wasn't limping as I ran. I made my way back home and decided to talk to Mary at first light.

It was Monday morning and there was a lot to do around the Proctor house, but I needed to get things straight before the day got started.

"Mary, Mary, wake up."

I shook her.
"What is it?"

She sat up with a start.
"I talked to Mr. Proctor last night."
"Did he visit you in your dreams? Is he haunting you, too?"
"Mary, stop being such a dork. I went to the jail and talked to Elizabeth and John. They are VERY worried about you. You must help me set them free by testifying for them. We must convince the magistrates that they never practiced witchcraft."

She just stared at me with her mouth open.

"Mary, Mary! Do you hear me? Are you listening? If we don't help them they will be hanged." I grabbed her by the shoulders.
"Maddie, I made you something."

She grinned like an idiot.

"What in the world are you talking about?"

"I made you a poppet, you know a doll. Look here it is." She wiggled out of my hands and reached under her bed. She handed me the doll made out of straw and sticks and cloth. "See, see, it looks like me."

"Mary, we don't have time for dolls and games. You have got to pay attention here."

I snatched the poppet away from her. A loud rapping on the door interrupted our conversation. I heard the voices of men and the trampling of feet.

"Is Mary Warren in there? Open this door...I say, open this door immediately!"

More pounding.

I hurriedly left Mary's room, and she followed in her bedclothes. Before I could even open it, the door burst open and there stood the constable with some other men from the village. They rushed in and grabbed Mary from behind me.

"Mary Warren, you are accused of tormenting Ann Putnam, Mercy Lewis, Mary Walcott and Elizabeth Hubbard! An official complaint has been entered against you."

Mary collapsed in their arms, screaming as she was dragged away.

"Maddie, Maddie save me!"

When the door slammed I stared hard in disbelief. But I wasn't staring at the door. I was staring at the simple, straw doll in my hands that Mary had made. My hands were shaking. The two unblinking eyes of the poppet stared back at me. Those eyes were orange beads with the familiar clear liquid floating inside flecked with specks of silver and gold. But they were so much more than just beads. Oh, so much more. They were my ticket out of this living hell of witches and specters and the evil that surrounded and engulfed Salem Village.

I excitedly tore the bead off the doll's head and got ready to pop it into my mouth. 21st century, here I come. Just then one of the younger Proctor boys entered the room and ask me what all the commotion was about. I comforted him and sent him to get dressed. I went back to my room and sat on the bed and started thinking really hard.

The Proctors were in jail waiting to stand trial. Now Mary was accused and arrested. I slowly realized that I couldn't just up and leave without trying to save the Proctors. If Mary ended up testifying against them, then I was the only eyewitness who could tell the truth about what had really gone on in this household. The only thing standing between the Proctors and the gallows was me. I couldn't just leave them to die after all they had done for me.

I hid both the poppet and the bead in my room for the time being. At least I knew if things got a little hairy I could exit Salem in a hurry. I almost laughed when I imagined what they would think if I disappeared right in front of their eyes. Limping Wolf Witch Girl vanishes!

I needed to talk to John Proctor again, but I found out he and Elizabeth had been taken to Boston while they awaited trial. There was no way I could get to Boston right now. Once again I stayed as far away from town as I could, but it was impossible not to hear the grim news. Mary Warren had gone absolutely berserk and had testified that the Proctors had made her sign the devil's book. She even admitted she was a witch and had tormented the others. I got more and more nervous with each passing day. How long before this nut job accused me as well? I kept the poppet with the magic bead on my person at all times, just in case I needed to make a quick getaway.

Nine more were accused. Then, another six were arrested. The wildfire spread outside of Salem Village and into the surrounding communities. No one was safe from the afflicted groups' far reaching accusations. Would I ever wake up from this nightmare?

We finally found out that John and Elizabeth Proctor were going to be tried on August 2nd. That was a long time to wait, but I passed the time helping John's oldest son take care of the boys. It was a big job, but I was the only one left to do most of the work. We somehow got a petition together that over fifty people signed, saying that none of them ever suspected the Proctors of witchcraft. I started hoping that this, combined with my testimony might be enough to save them.

On the afternoon of July 19th I heard the saddest, most depressing news I had ever heard since I came to this terrible place. That morning, Sarah Good, Rebecca Nurse and three other women had been hanged at the gallows in the public square of Salem Village. I heard the crowds were so thick, the cart that carried the victims could barely get through. As I cried, I wondered if this terrible event would bring the girls to their senses or drive them on to even more terrible acts. Had they passed the point of no return? The others awaiting trial had to now know that their prospects were grim.

The fateful day of the trial finally arrived and I forced myself to attend. The courtroom was packed even tighter than the last time I was there. Things went pretty much as I expected. All of the afflicted girls testified against Mr. Proctor which came as no surprise. None of them dared make eye contact with me. The big news came from Mary Warren. Just as I had heard, she testified that John Proctor had forced her to sign the black book. She said that the Proctors had tortured her, threatened to drown her and to burn her with hot pokers from the fireplace. I just slowly shook my head at this complete nonsense. Just let me at them.

John Proctor looked like a beaten man. He was haggard and worn from his lengthy prison stay. He didn't have much to say except that he was not ready to die. He also said that he knew that some of the people who had confessed, including Mary, had been tied and beaten and their property taken away. I could barely stand to see him so forlorn. The only bright spot was when the petition was presented that his neighbors signed saying they never saw him performing witchcraft.

His trial was winding down, and I knew it was now or never. I gathered all of my courage and stood up.

"Excuse me, sirs." No one heard me.

"JOHN PROCTOR IS NO MORE OF A WITCH THAN ALL OF YOU!"

That got everyone's attention.

"Excuse me, Miss...?"
"Your honors, my name is Maddie Tucker and I would like to speak on behalf of John Proctor."
"That is highly unusual. I assume you have had the chance to sign the petition?"
"Yes, I have signed it, but I have personal knowledge of the accused since I lived with him as his servant for about five months. I know that Mary Warren is lying."

The courtroom lay completely still and silent.

"One moment, please."

The magistrates conferred for a few minutes and then agreed to let me testify. I was sworn in and they questioned me.
"Tell us then, Maggie, what is it that you have seen?"
"The name is MADDIE, and those girls over there are all a bunch of rotten liars."

I pointed towards them and gave them my best stare. For once they looked like they were on trial.

I told the judges all about the meeting that fateful, cold night in January in the Parris' kitchen. I told them all about the egg white in the glass and how Ann Putnam has scared Betty Parris half to death with her story about how Betty was going to be a bride of death. I told them how Reverend Parris had beaten the confession out of Tituba. I told them how mixed-up and scared that Mary

Warren was, and that she was only trying to save her neck by accusing other people. Mostly I told them what a good man John Proctor was, and how he and his family had taken me in when I had no where else to go. I told them that even though John Proctor was gruff and rash, and that he didn't really like Reverend Parris, that I never EVER, EVER saw anything that even remotely looked like witchcraft in his household. I told them that even though Mr. Proctor had a bad temper, he was innocent of being a witch.

Finally, I turned toward the gaggle of accusers at the side of room, sitting there with there mouths wide open like they were in shock. I stepped toward them and pointed at them.

"And you, you all should be ashamed at all the trouble you have caused with your foolishness. You frauds have sent innocent people to prison, you have separated children from their mothers, and you have caused people's property to be taken from them."

I was rolling now.

"And worst of all, the very worst of all your evil...PEOPLE HAVE DIED BECAUSE OF YOUR LIES!!! May their blood be on your hands."

I turned to John Proctor and saw him wipe a tear from his eyes. I thought I heard someone say, "Amen, sister", but it was mostly quiet.

Mary Putnam's scream slashed through the dead air like a knife and pierced my soul. As I spun I saw her falling on her knees and pointing to the ceiling.

"It is Maddie on the beam! There she sits with her yellow birds and suckling cats and the Devil's black book. She comes for us!"

As one, Mercy Lewis, Mary Walcott, and Elizabeth Hubbard slid off their chairs and started wailing and crying and pointing to the ceiling. There wasn't squat up there, but of course everyone looked anyway. I couldn't let them get away with it. I rushed toward them.

"Stop it, stop it, STOP IT NOW! You know there isn't anything up there. Look at me, I'm standing right here in front of you."

I reached out to grab one of them. They all recoiled in horror, screeching like banshees.

"See she comes for us. Save us, save us, please, please. We will not sign your book!"

Elizabeth Hubbard ran toward the judges.

"Your honors, she is one of them! She told us she flies like a witch! She told us she could see into the future!"

Not good. Now all the others chimed in.

"She told us about flying in shiny metal tubes and riding in metal boxes."

The magistrates were now eyeing me suspiciously.

"She told us we would be able to talk to each other from miles and miles away. She said we could hear music in our ears at anytime and that we would never be hungry or cold." "Do they speak the truth Maddie Tucker?"

I stammered.

"Well,...sirs, your honors...um, I can't really remember exactly what I said, and I may have said something just a little bit like that, but I was just kidding around and trying to have some fun."

The girls pressed their advantage.

"She comes to us in the night and whispers evil in our ears. She pinches us and chokes us and forces us to sign her black book. But we won't, we never will sign it!"

This was quickly spiraling out of control. I had to think of something fast. I turned to Mary and pleaded with her.

"Mary, Mary, tell them. Tell them it is all just a big mistake. That we, you and me, and all the other girls were just trying to have some fun on a cold night. Tell them that you all are just trying to get a little attention. Tell them to stop this madness!"

Mary slowly rose to her feet and every eye in the courtroom was on her. A smile gradually spread across her face. She lifted her shirt and revealed several red welts on her belly. She whispered hoarsely and deliberately.

"Maddie Tucker fashioned a poppet in my likeness. She hid it under my bed. She uses it every day to torment me. When she stabs the poppet with a needle, I feel it."

For emphasis she doubled over in pain. I stared at her in disbelief.

"Sirs, I have no idea of what she is talking about."

I raised my two hands, palms upward beside me. At that very second, the doll she had made me, the doll in my pocket I had forgotten about, the doll that held the sacred bead, the bead that was my escape pod out of Salem and back to the future, that doll fell silently out of my pocket and tumbled onto the floor. Oh, boy.

"SEIZE HER AND THE POPPET!"

The magistrate thundered.

"Maddie Tucker you are accused of witchcraft and will be examined on the morrow!"

I stooped down and made a quick move to try to get to the doll and the bead, but the constable grabbed my arms just before I reached it. I watched in dismay as Mary Warren curtsied to me, and then handed my passport to freedom to the judge. His eyebrows arched as he dramatically pulled a needle from the doll's side. GASP!

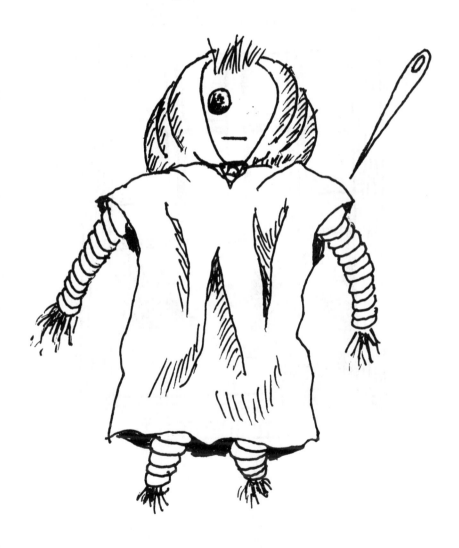

Chapter 10
FLIGHT

My confused brain immediately switched into overdrive. I had done everything I could to try and save John Proctor. I had stayed longer in Salem than I should have. Where had that needle come from? There was no way I was going to be able to talk myself out of this one. I had no chance of saving myself, let alone John Proctor. My only hope was to try to get one of those beads and get the heck out of Salem. Where had the needle come from? I had seen the heavy chains that were used to hold the accused and knew I could never get out of one of those babies. Forget about the needle, forget about Mary Warren, forget about everything except getting one of those beads in my mouth. The time to act was....NOW!

I pulled my arms together and put my fists up to my face. Just like I had learned in tai kwan do, I made a rapid downward motion with my arms bringing my elbows out beside me. I broke the grip of the constable and continued spinning to my left. As I did I bent my left arm, pulled it in and then let it swing around with all the force I could muster. Luckily my elbow landed right in the middle of his soft gut and you could audibly hear the air escape as he grunted. Connection! When he doubled over I brought my right knee up to his groin and then stomped on his left foot as hard as I could. He fell over sideways with a loud thud. I looked up and noticed that everyone's mouths were wide open in amazement. I guess they had never seen a witch fight back before.

I held my arms open wide and gave them my scariest face.

"That's right, I'm a witch from the future and I'm about to put a curse on all of you! The only thing you people of Salem will ever be remembered for is killing a bunch of innocent people!"

The natives were getting restless. I saw Reverend Proctor whispering something to Mr. Putnam. I only had a few more seconds. I turned to the magistrate.

"Now hand over that doll, sir, and I give you my word you will NEVER see me again!"

I strode over to him, grabbed the doll out of his trembling hand and inched toward the open window a few feet away. The door was blocked with people. I could see Parris and Putnam moving toward me. I held the doll out toward them.

"Stay back! I'm warning you, stay back."

I fumbled with the bead on the doll, but I couldn't tear it loose. My hands were sweating like crazy.

"BACK!"

I needed to get outside to buy more time to get the bead loose. I gave them one more sneer, put the doll in my mouth and dove out the open window. Stop, drop and roll.

It was further to the ground than I had calculated, and I landed awkwardly rolling over and over. The doll flew out of my mouth. They were at the window and already coming out of the door screaming and shouting. I grabbed the doll and started hobbling around the building as fast as I could go. Now in addition to my knee, my wrist was also killing me. I didn't care. I just was going to tear that bead off with my teeth and disappear from Salem forever. I just about fainted when I looked down at the doll and saw the bead was not there. What the...?! It must have fallen off when I hit the ground. I started back and saw about thirty very angry, full grown men chasing after me. Dog poopie!

No way was I going to outrun them with my bad leg. It certainly would have been nice if I could actually fly. I had to hide. Where? Where? Where? I kept moving and came to the jail where they held the prisoners. Suddenly I thought I heard someone calling my name.

"Hey, Maddie, over here."
"What?"
"Over here. Hide in this barrel. Quick before they catch you."

I thought I recognized the voice, but his sketchy face was hidden by the shadows. The only thing I could tell for sure is that he was wearing a cape. I wasn't sure I could trust him, but I was pretty much out of options. He held the barrel sideways while I squeezed myself in.

"Just keep quiet and I'll take care of everything."

I heard the posse come around the corner huffing and puffing just as he slammed the lid shut. I listened to the muffled conversation.

"You there, sir, where did she go?"
"Who?"
"A young girl."
"How young?"
"Twelve or thirteen maybe."
"Name?"
"Maddie."
"Maggie?"
"NO, MADDIE!"
"Can't say I've seen anyone lately?"
"She just came around this corner not more than a minute ago."
"Sorry."
"She was limping and carrying a doll."
"Oh, THAT girl."
"Yes, that girl. Which way did she go?"
"You wouldn't believe me if I told you."
"Well?"
"She flew away on a broom right over those trees there."

A long silence.
"Oh, and one more thing."
"What's that?"
"She was laughing."

I heard the men talking for a few more minutes and then everything went quiet. I stayed in the cramped, smelly barrel for as long as I could stand it, but I finally just had to get out of there. When I pushed the lid open it was dark and I didn't see anyone else around. I crawled out of the barrel and slunk over to the nearest woods. No sign of the constable yet.

While I was squatting in the barrel I realized I had little or no chance of finding the bead outside of the meetinghouse. My best bet was to return to the Proctor's house and retrieve the other bead from the doll I had hidden earlier. I carefully made my way through the dark woods back to the house. It was slow going, through the thick forest, but I was so intent on getting that bead I didn't even worry about the wolves or Indians.

When I finally got back to the Proctors, it was crawling with men from the village. I thought I saw the constable, Reverend Parris and Mr. Putnam prowling around. I knew they couldn't stay there forever, but I also knew I desperately needed to get inside, find the bead with the marker fluid and get back to the future. Desperate times call for desperate measures.

I stepped out of the woods just a little, cupped my hands around my mouth and yelled as loud as I could.

"HELP! HELP! THE INDIANS ARE ATTACKING. HEY, EVERYBODY! THE INDIANS ARE ATTACKING RIGHT OVER HERE! HELP! HELP! HELP!"

It didn't take long for my little strategy to pay off. Big time. The men came running and I doubled back around the house. I knew I only had a minute or two to find the bead and make my exit. I slipped in quietly through the back door and raced up the stairs to my room. Now where did I put it? Think! Think! I looked everywhere. Under my bed, in my dresser, in my closet. Where was that darn orange bead? Then I heard a sinister, evil laugh.

"Looking for this, little Miss Witch?"

Reverend Parris stood in the doorway with an evil grin spreading slowly across his face. He was holding the bead between his thumb and index finger. Dadgummit.

"Not everyone fell for your sneaky Indian ploy."
"OK, Reverend Parris. Just give me that bead and you'll never see or hear from me again. I promise."
"That's rich, the word of a witch."
"Just give me the bead. NOW!"

I lunged at him and the bead, but he stepped to the side and pushed me down to the ground. When he pushed me though, the bead fell from his hand and rolled down the hallway. I scrambled after it, but he tackled me.

"Oh, no you don't. You're not getting away this time."

We wrestled in the hallway for a couple of seconds and I somehow managed to bite his hand really hard. He howled in pain and let go for just a second. That gave me enough space to give him a swift kick in the head and he grabbed his face in obvious pain. I jumped up and ran into the Proctors bedroom, the last place I had seen the bead rolling. Parrish was up on his knees grunting and I heard more noise downstairs. I guess they had figured out that Indians weren't attacking. Parrish yelled.

"She's up here. The witch just bit me."

Hope he was bleeding. A lot. I slammed the door of the bedroom, and pushed the dresser in front of it. Where's that bead? It was almost pitch black, so I almost had no chance of finding it. What I needed was more time. Just then I remembered something amazing about the house that John Proctor had shown me when I first started living there. Because of the constant fear of Indian attacks, Mr. Proctor had built secret hidden steps behind the fireplace that led to downstairs. Just like the House of the Seven Gables, the Proctor's house had a mysterious secret stairway. Now if I could only remember how to get to it.

I ran to the fireplace and frantically searched the nearby wall for the false panel. Parris was banging into the door, forcing his way into the room. The dresser fell with a crash, just as the wall panel rotated. I slipped into the darkness, and flipped the panel in one motion. When Parris entered the room he found it completely witch free. The panel groove left just enough space for me to see into the darkened room. Mr. Putnam and the constable followed on his heels. They were all breathing hard.

"She has vanished into the night."

They went to the window.

"More light! More light!"

Candles were lit and they searched every square inch of the room.

"She's not here. She flew away again just like she did near the jail."

Parris had a disgusted look on his face.

"I know she's in this house somewhere. Keep looking!"

As I watched them leave the room, I saw something that made my heart leap up into my throat. About two feet from the secret panel I saw the last orange bead sparkling slightly, right in the middle of the floor! If I knelt down and stretched I could probably reach it. I had to get to it, before the men came back and discovered it. I crouched down and turned the panel about two inches. It creaked ever so slightly. I stretched out my right arm as far as I could go and of course it was just out of reach. I pressed my body up against the wall and walked my fingers to the bead. Ummmmmmm. GOT IT!

Reverend Parris' boot came smashing down on my already injured wrist and pinned my arm to the floor. The pain almost made me pass out. The bead trickled out of my fingertips and I looked at Parris as I tumbled into the room. He threw back his head, cackling as I screamed. It wasn't pain though, that made me scream. It was the horror of watching in utter hopelessness as my future disappeared. With his boot heel he slowly and deliberately ground the orange bead into the floor.

Chapter 11
FUTURE SHOCK

The conditions at the Salem Jail were downright disgusting. They didn't even bother to waste any time with another sham preliminary hearing. The magistrates set my case for trial and slapped me in leg irons in about ten seconds. The Salem jail could have easily doubled as a torture chamber in a horror movie. It was cold and dark and they kept us chained to the walls so our "specters" would be less inclined to visit "the afflicted." The really exciting news was that we had lots and lots of rats for company.

After I sat in that horrible place for a couple of days, one of the lady jailers searched me up and down looking for witch marks. How she could tell the witch marks from the numerous rat bites was a complete mystery to me. We were given almost no food and water, so we would be more likely to confess. Here's the best part. They billed me for the little food I ate and for salaries of the magistrates, jailer and the hangman. I guess someone had to pay for these luxurious accommodations. If I really was a witch I would have flown out and brought back pizza for everyone.

On August 19th, five more people were hanged as witches on Gallow's Hill. Sadly, one of them was John Proctor. I spent most of the day crying and trying to figure out how everything had gone so badly. The most impressive thing was that almost none of the accused confessed to being a witch. These Puritans of Salem were obviously a tough bunch. If they had only "confessed" like Mary Warren they could have been home sleeping in their own beds and enjoying their lives. Evidently they were willing to die rather than confess to something they didn't do. The only good news on that depressing day was that Elizabeth Proctor was pregnant and would not be hanged until she had her baby. I guess the Puritans figured the baby couldn't be a witch. Yet.

There was little or no opportunity for escape, so my only chance was to prove that I wasn't a witch at my trial and survive long enough to try and get home. All and all it looked pretty bleak. The date of my trial was rapidly approaching and the jail was filling up with more and more of the accused. Eleven people had been hanged so far and there was no end in sight. I spent a lot of time chewing on my fingernails and worrying. Even though I didn't want to be hanged, I would never confess to being a witch even though that was probably the easiest thing to do.

When the date of my trial finally arrived I hadn't really come up with any earth shattering ideas on how to defend myself. It had been so long since I had seen sunlight, I just stood there blinking when they brought me into the room. As usual the courtroom was packed with the curious and the bloodthirsty. I guess the news of my attempted escape had spread and I was a celebrity witch by now. I couldn't think of one single solitary person in Salem who would testify on my behalf. All of my real friends were either dead or in prison.

The usual gaggle of "afflicted" girls and women stood to the side pretending to be afraid of me. I stamped at them and rattled my leg irons just to scare them a little. They acted like I had stabbed them with a butcher knife. The magistrate pounded his gavel and brought the hearing to order.

"Maddie Tucker, you are accused of practicing witchcraft and further stand accused of being in a league with the devil, having signed his book, having urged and threatened others to sign his book, and of torturing and afflicting others by various and sundry methods of wicked activity. What say you?"

I'm not exactly certain what he just accused me of, and I was about to open my mouth to defend myself when the door blew open and I saw the single most amazing thing I have ever seen in my entire short life. There standing in the doorway in a powdered wig and a light-blue crushed velvet Pilgrim's outfit, complete with black buckled boots like one of the three musketeers and a black cape was...you're not going to believe this...someone who looked suspiciously like...MY DAD!

My jaw dropped open along with everyone else's as he slammed the door and strode across the room to the table behind me. With dramatic flair he whirled off his cape and flung it on the table and came and stood beside me. Holy time travel, Batman.

"Dad? Is that you? Omigosh! What?...When?...How in the heck....Where in all of creation did you get that...that...outfit?"

He whispered out of the side of his mouth.

"It was the only one I could find at the costume store. Now just keep your mouth shut and follow my lead and maybe we can both get out of here in one piece."

He gave me a big popeyed wink.

"Nice wig, Dad."

"May it please the court, good sirs..."

"Sir, this is highly irregular. This is a proceeding of the court of Oyer and Terminer and will not be interrupted by any foolishness of any sort. Now stand down and find a seat or you will be removed."

"But sirs I am a lawyer and I wish to be recognized and heard by this court."

"State your name and your business then."

"I am...er...Hamilton Burger...a barrister from Boston and I am here to defend my....my....er niece. Yes, that's it, my niece...uh..., Maggie Tucker, I mean Maddie Tucker, on the charges of (aside to me) What exactly have they charged you with, babe?"

81

"You name it. They charged me with it."

"Sir?"

"Yes against whatever it is this fine court has charged her with, to wit, the charges levied against her today, this very hour, right here and....uh, right now. This very second."

"Ahem. I have both practiced law and sat on this judicial bench for many years in the Boston locale and have never heard of you, Mr. Hamilton...what was that again?"

"Burger."

"Burger?"

"That's right, perhaps you may have heard of my firm, Ham, Burger and Cheese?"

When I saw that slight smile creep across his face, I knew I was in a lot of trouble. Here was my Dad trying to be funny while MY LIFE WAS HANGING IN THE BALANCE. The last thing I needed was for him to be smack talking a bunch of humorless Puritan judges who were itching to string me up. Fortunately they didn't catch the humor.

"Regardless, you may proceed."

They read the charges again. I tried to catch my Dad's eye, but he was in full lawyer mode. I knew my dad was a lawyer, but I haven't actually ever seen him practicing law. He mostly sits at his computer typing e-mails and scratching himself. I didn't know if he was any good at it.

"To begin, sirs, we would request a continuance, so I can further consult with my client."

"Mr. Burger. There will be no continuances. We have five more cases to try today, so let's get on with it."

"I wish to have my objection noted for the record."

The judge sighed.

"So noted."

The magistrates trotted out each of the girls who had been at the Parris house that fateful night, one by one. Of course they accused me of practicing voodoo, predicting the future, practicing witchcraft, trying to get them to sign the book, afflicting them with my specter, blah, blah, blah. Each testimony was strikingly similar. I have to admit it, Dad did a great job of cross-examining them, pointing out inconsistencies in their stories. None of them recanted their lies, but he poked a lot of holes in their testimony. Without fail, whenever he would back them into a corner they would go into their crazy victim routine and pretend like I was attacking them. I hoped the jury was noticing how foolish they looked. Morons.

Dad even caught one of the screaming girls hiding a needle in her clothing. He demonstrated to the jury how easy it was to stab himself with it and make it look like someone had attacked him. The tide was starting to turn.

By the time he questioned Mary Warren, she must have gotten the message. She pretended like she couldn't see or hear anything just to get out of testifying. This was actually going a lot better than I expected. She obviously wasn't testifying, so that pretty much wrapped it up for the prosecution. I guess Pops didn't want to call me, because he just launched into his closing argument. He probably figured he couldn't risk me getting fired up and saying something stupid. He stared down the all male jury.

"Gentlemen. Good Sirs. Honorable members of the jury. I ask you to consider today not just the case of this poor unfortunate child, but also all of those who have come before you and all who will come before you. Most of those charged are defenseless women, the poor, the mentally ill, the elderly and the dispossessed. Many have been held without even being charged and none of them before today have had the benefit of counsel. The testimony you have used to convict those now hanged includes hearsay, contradictory statements, and blatant lies. Worst of all most you have accepted as truth the most questionable of all evidence: spectral evidence. You have taken the word of mere girls who claim to see things that no one else sees to convict some of the finest folks that have ever walked the streets of Salem. Anyone who is an outsider or disliked can be charged, convicted, and hanged for witchcraft in a mere matter of weeks."

Dad took a dramatic pause and slowly walked the length of the courtroom. The jurors watched him every step of the way. He had them.

"Perhaps some day Salem will become part of a great nation. Imagine if you will, a nation where it will be unlawful to hold people without charging them, where everyone charged will have the benefit of legal representation and where a person may only be convicted by demonstrable evidence that is beyond a reasonable doubt. Isn't that the kind of nation you would wish to call your own? Is it not true that the best of your belief states that you are to love your neighbor as yourself? Where has that love gone in Salem?"

The room was deathly quiet. Dad drew a deep breath.

"This future nation will be conceived in liberty and dedicated to the proposition that all men and women are created equal, and that all, regardless of their race, religion or creed have the right to life, liberty and the pursuit of happiness. The world will little note or long remember what is said here today, but it will never forget those who died in Salem. We should rather resolve that those who died here did not die in vain, but that justice for the people and by the people shall not perish from the earth..."

84

Hey wait a minute. This all sounded vaguely familiar. Didn't Dad just rip off Thomas Jefferson and Abraham Lincoln all in the same breath? He continued now, his voice swelling with emotion.

"...So now I ask you men of Salem, ask not, ask not what Salem can do for you. Ask what you can do for Salem!"

He stamped his foot and gave a broad gesture.

"You see, gentlemen of the jury, I have a dream..."

Dad was riffing on history, stealing material from every great American statesmen and orator he could remember.

"...a dream where every valley shall be exalted, every hill and mountain laid low, every crooked place made straight, and where everyone shall be free at last, free at last. So now in conclusion, I beg you to look within and ask yourselves if there is enough evidence here today to convict Maddie Tucker of witchcraft? Probably just as much as you have used to convict the others you have already hanged. But mark my words, people of Salem, history will judge you harshly for the evils you have committed in this very room. Now is your chance to change that unholy past, to make history and to begin anew. Let Maddie Tucker go free and she will return with me to Boston and you will never see either of us again."

Way to go, Dad! Not too shabby for a guy wearing a horrendous looking light blue suit and the most ridiculous powdered wig in the history of headgear. I was actually optimistic when the jury shuffled out to consider the evidence. My accusers all sat silently, and frankly they looked worried to me. I tried to talk to my Dad during the break, but he just put a finger to his lips and shook his head. Everyone in the audience was whispering and looking at us and occasionally pointing. I was starting to get really uncomfortable when the jury finally strode back in. None of them looked at me. The head guy handed the written verdict to the chief magistrate. The judge carefully opened it, read it and looked straight at me. Expressionless. He showed it to the other two judges and there was a brief but fierce whispering match among them. Finally the one in the middle stood slowly. We all rose with him. My heart was beating so loudly I thought everyone could hear it. Dad held my hand and I could see he had his fingers crossed behind his back.

"The jury has spoken. Maddie Tucker is...."

Chapter 12

TIME FLIES WHEN YOU'RE HANGING
"...ahem..."

Well, just spit it out, pal. Come on, come on...
"...not guilty."

One Mississippi...two Mississippi...three Mississippi...then the room was engulfed in a tsunami of chaos. First me and my dad are hugging each other and jumping up and down like idiots. He grabs me by the waist with one hand and his cape with the other and starts twirling it around and around. Then he drops me, runs around the table and starts high-fiving anybody else in the near vicinity. I guess by the looks of things, he had never actually won a case before.

Next, the crowd is going absolutely berserk. Everyone is shouting and screaming and it sounded like the inside of fifth grade on the last day of school. Papers are flying, people are running in and out and everyone is shouting. The jury members are shaking hands and smacking each other on the back. All three magistrates are up pounding on their table trying to restore order. They looked incredibly unhappy.

I took a second just to glance over at my accusers. They all looked like someone had just stolen their dog. I guess they realized their evil spell over Salem had finally been broken. For once, no one in the room was paying one bit of attention to them. I felt like wagging my finger in their faces and shaking my booty, but I was just relieved that this was finally over. Then I saw all of them gather in a little huddle with Ann Putnam right in the middle. And then it hit me. I grabbed Dad by the arm.

"Pops, we have got to get out of here."

I started dragging him to the door.

"Right, now!"

But it was too late. Ann Putnam, Mary Warren and all the others had thrown themselves on the floor and were twisting and writhing like they never had before. They screamed, and scratched their arms and faces. The judges, pounding on the table, finally restored calm, and of course everyone was once again completely focused on the girls. They played it for all it was worth, pretending I was attacking them again. When I saw how crazy they were acting I knew I would never get out of Salem alive. These nut-jobs were not going to be stopped.

Sure enough, after the judges had a brief pow-wow, the head magistrate ask the jury to go back out and reconsider the verdict. Of course they weren't gone very long THIS time. They obviously got the message because when they came back in, the new verdict was, you guessed it, guilty. Dad threw out every argument he could think of and made every motion he knew, but nothing could change the judges' final decision. Maddie Tucker was to be hanged by the neck until dead, in three days at Gallows Hill. When they dragged me kicking and screaming out of that courtroom, Dad just shrugged his shoulders and gave me a little wave. He pounded on his heart twice and pointed at me.

The jail was darker and even more depressing than ever. Probably because I thought I was never going to be back here, and that I actually was going to be leaving Salem. Oh, I was going to be leaving Salem, all right. In a pine box evidently. Since I was a well known escape risk, they watched me like a hawk. Even if I could manage to get out of these leg irons and chains I knew I wouldn't get too far. Besides that, my knee was hurting again from all the jumping around I did after my trial, and my wrist was just killing me. All in all things were looking pretty bleak.

My only hope was Dad. Since he was here in Salem, he had to be doing everything he could to get me out of this terrible mess. I mean he was pretty good at fixing things and solving problems, right? Right?

"Hey, Dad."

"Maddie, you are not allowed to bother me when I'm watching televison."

"You're always watching television."

"Exactly."

"Dad my X-box is broken."

"What's an X-box?"

"That thing in my room that plays games."

"Your brother is in your room?"

"Try to focus here, Dad. The X-box plays dvds and video games. It cost $300 and you got it for me last Christmas. It's not working."

"I spent $300 on YOU?"

"DAD!"

"Is it plugged in?"

"Duh."

"Is it turned on?"

Sigh. "Yes."

"And it's not working."

"No."

"Sounds like it's broken. Excuse me, Maggie. The game is back on. Hey, by the way, can you program my cell phone for me? Thanks."

Ok, maybe Dad wasn't so hot with technology, but this was more like a rescue mission. I was trying to recall if he remembered to wear his glasses. He was blind as a bat without them. Not good.

The three days before my scheduled execution passed quickly. No visitors, no last minute pardon from the governor and no sign of Dad anywhere. I was beginning to wonder if this was really going to be it for me. Twelve years old and I hadn't even got to do all those fun things that teenagers get to do. I'm not really sure what they are, but they had to be way better than getting hanged by the neck.

The morning of my impending death arrived without fanfare. They didn't really say at my sentencing what time the execution was supposed to be, so each minute that passed was filled with agony. I thought about my family, my life, and the markers. If Dad could just show up anytime he wanted then where in the heck was he right now, the very time that I needed him the most? I was sick to my stomach and filled with dread. Finally, right before sunset, they came to get me. I was too numb to struggle.

Gallows Hill was just a little bit outside of town. It was practically the highest point around. I guess they wanted to make certain everyone had a really good view. They led me out of the jail into the late afternoon sun. The shadows created that eerie half light that makes you feel like you are traveling between two worlds. Other than the fact that I was about to die, it was a glorious day. The road to the hill was filled with just about everyone from the county. I guess everybody wanted to see the dramatic ending of "Wolf Witch Girl from the Future." I recognized a few familiar faces, but mostly only strangers bore witness to my final minutes on Earth.

As the wagon rolled slowly along, mud flying from its wheels, I tried to imagine that I was a queen on the way to her coronation. These gawkers were my loyal subjects and the moths and early fireflies surrounding me were the flowers they tossed at my feet. I squinted and tried my best not to cry. I wasn't going to give any of them that satisfaction.

By the time we got to the gallows, the crowd was so thick the wagon could barely get through. They removed my leg irons and led me slowly up the steps. The sun was setting and it was almost like a dream. Someone tied my hands behind my back and I caught a glimpse of Reverend Parris' smirking face in the crowd. I barely noticed that the rope wasn't as tight as it should have been. Everyone was still and silent as the charges against me were read aloud. I could see the rough noose hanging just in front of me and the trap door at my feet. Someone asked me if I had any last words. I didn't even answer.

They shoved me forward and the noose fell around my neck. The noose tightened. My executioner reached for the lever to open the trap door. The last hint of sunlight faded from the sky. I closed my eyes. A deep breath. A gust of wind.

That's when I first heard it. A distance sound of thunder. Growing louder. Louder still. I knew that sound. It was the unmistakable pounding of hoof beats on hard ground. I opened my eyes and saw a headless horseman flying through the crowd, black cape flowing around him, a whip in one hand and a flaming pumpkin (are you kidding me?) in the other. The throng parted like a wave crashing on the shore, scattering in every direction. I glanced at my executioner. He was undeterred. I started working on the rope behind me. He pulled the lever just as I tore my hands free from my bindings. As the trap door opened below me, I grabbed the noose with both hands and broke my fall. I hung there dangling and kicking in midair when the flaming pumpkin crashed onto the platform in a hail of fire and pumpkin guts.

The stunned executioner fell back in fear as the headless horseman leaped from his steed onto the platform. He cracked his whip again and again, furiously holding back the crowd. Then he turned, grabbed me by the waist and tore the noose from around my neck.

"Come on Maddie, let's show these country bumpkins some real magic!"
"DAD!"
"Do you realize that you have the most beautiful face?"
"What!?"
"Let's blow this popsicle stand and give these Pilgrims a taste of their own medicine. They want witchcraft? Will give 'em something they'll never forget."
"Dad, they're Puritans."
"What?"
"Never mind. What's the plan?"
"I don't really have one. Just follow my lead."
"Dad, where are your glasses?"
"They must have fallen off somewhere."

He pulled another smaller pumpkin out of his cloak, lit it with a torch and fired it into the crowd. The executioner was snapping out of his fog, so Dad grabbed me by the waist again and we leaped onto the waiting horse. I heard a distinct grunt from Dad when we landed. He spurred the horse, cracked his whip one last time and we sped into the night. I held on for dear life. I saw Reverend Parris and Mr. Putnam swinging into action. They weren't going to just sit idly by and let me escape again.

To my great dismay I realized the horse was slowing down. Somehow Dad had managed to borrow a plow horse for his daring rescue. He was out of gas. Great. We slid down off the horse, Dad took my hand and we hit the ground running into the dark woods. A wolf howled in the distance. The good men of Salem had reorganized and were in hot pursuit. Their torches lit up the forest like the Fourth of July.

"Not to worry, Maddie. I've got a couple of beads hidden with me somewhere. Now where did I put them?'

"You're just messing with me right, Dad?"

"RUN, MADDIE, RUN!"

I stripped down to my long underwear, since my stupid dress kept getting caught on the thorns and bushes. Did I mention that my knee was about to explode from pain? Dad kept dragging me along.

This was really a funny time to recall a conversation I had with Pops not too long before my trip. Dad was the original absent minded professor.

"Maddie, we have got to go. Have you seen my car keys?"

"Would they be different from the ones you are holding in your hand right now?"

"Oh. Ok, I just need to find my glasses and we can look frosty."

"You mean the ones YOU ARE WEARING?"
"Yeah, those, I guess maybe."

Dad was stripping off clothes, running for his life, patting his pockets and looking for the beads all at the same time. If our lives weren't in so much danger it would have been hilarious. We kept tripping on the underbrush. The Puritans were closing in. They finally surrounded us at a clearing near the edge of a cliff. There we were, both sweating and bleeding, standing in our long underwear. Parris and Putnam stepped forward just as the wolves burst into the circle growling and snarling like, like, well, like a pack of starving wolves. They must have been so hungry they weren't even afraid of the fire the men carried. Perfect timing!

Dad had the most wonderful look on his face. He gently pulled two marvelous, magnificent, magical, orange beads out of his shirt pocket and smiled at me. The translucent liquid in the beads glowed in the flickering torchlight. He cautiously handed me one bead, taking great care not to drop it. A wolf advanced. Putnam raised a musket. Dad wagged his index finger back and forth at all of them. Not today. He looked at me and I looked at him. We swallowed the beads, held hands, leaped off the cliff, soaring into that dark New England night, flying like witches back into the future. I guarantee you, they never found our bodies.

Ouch, ouch, ouch. OUCH! The bumping was just killing my knee and my wrist wasn't much better. The tight stretcher straps pinned down my arms and legs.

"Hey, take it easy!."

"Maddie, thank goodness you're awake. How are you feeling?"

"What?"

"You had a pretty nasty fall coming down the mountain. I think you twisted your knee and maybe broke your wrist. You were unconscious and we had to request a mountain rescue. We'll be down to the bottom in a few minutes."

"Sure, Dad. I guess you're going to tell me next that you've never worn a cape or a light blue Pilgrim's costume?"

"Wow, Maddie, you must have hit your head a lot harder than I thought. Why don't you just stay quiet and rest. You'll feel better after we get you to the hospital."

"Ok, then where are your glasses?"

"I must have left them at the hut."

"Right."

Fortunately nothing was broken, but I had to be on crutches for a few days. This obviously made the trip back to Florida a lot more complicated. I kept asking Dad to tell me about the markers, but he wouldn't ever answer me. He wouldn't admit he knew anything about them, but it was pretty clear that he's been in on it since the beginning. I was so happy to be alive and out of Salem, that I finally quit bugging him about it.

I spent a couple of days in Florida before I had to fly back to Atlanta. I thought a long time about the markers and my four trips back in time. Even though I had learned a few things, and had some great adventures, with each trip the journeys had gotten harder and harder. I decided I didn't really like history at all. It wasn't full of happy stories with happy endings like a lot of books I read. The tragedy I witnessed at Salem really opened my eyes to all the evil and sadness that seem to be the true history of the human race. These weren't magic markers that Dad had given me. They were tragic markers. I had experienced enough of history. More than enough. When it was time to go, I took my box of magic markers and left them in the trash can by the side of the road. Enough was enough.

As we pulled out of the driveway to go to the airport, I saw my little sister, Natalie, rummaging through the trash. She must have been looking for one of her ten million stuffed animals Dad is always trying to throw out. I gasped and pounded on the window when I saw her pull out the case of heavy, solid, reddish wood with solid brass hinges and a solid brass clasp. No way was my sweet, little Natalie going to survive time travel.